A mysterious

"The rumor going around is that a band of kids is mixed up in all this, kind of modern-day Robin Hoods."

A jolt went through me, made my knees go weak and stopped my breathing. My world shrank down to that narrow-eyed look outside and the wild panic inside. "Oh?" I said, my voice quite a bit higher than usual, up there in six-year-old range. I forced myself to breathe again, tried to get my voice back under control. "Really?" Really: the puniest response there was.

"That's the rumor." Did Dina's lips start curving up in that little smile? The nearest streetlight was out, so I couldn't be sure. "But if true, I'd have a sympathetic reaction, if you see what I mean."

"I don't."

"My coverage would be positive," Dina said. "Here's something you might not have realized—shown in the right light, those kids could be stars."

"Huh?"

"Why not? Wasn't Robin Hood a star?"

OTHER BOOKS YOU MAY ENJOY

Al Capone Does My Homework	Gennifer Choldenko
Al Capone Does My Shirts	Gennifer Choldenko
Al Capone Shines My Shoes	Gennifer Choldenko
The Books of Elsewhere: Volume 1: The Shadows	Jacqueline West
The Case of the Missing Marquess: An Enola Holmes Mystery	Nancy Springer
Gilda Joyce, Psychic Investigator	Jennifer Allison
The Outlaws of Sherwood Street: Stealing from the Rich	Peter Abrahams
Savvy	Ingrid Law
A Tale Dark & Grimm	Adam Gidwitz

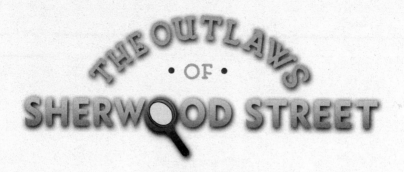

THE OUTLAWS • OF • SHERWOOD STREET

Giving to the Poor

PETER ABRAHAMS

PUFFIN BOOKS
An Imprint of Penguin Group (USA)

THIS ONE'S FOR MY DAD,

WHO TAUGHT ME THE NIGHT SKY.

PUFFIN BOOKS
Published by the Penguin Group
Penguin Group (USA) LLC
375 Hudson Street
New York, New York 10014

USA * Canada * UK * Ireland * Australia
New Zealand * India * South Africa * China

penguin.com
A Penguin Random House Company

First published in the United States of America by Philomel Books, 2013
Published by Puffin Books, an imprint of Penguin Young Readers Group, 2014

Edited by Jill Santopolo. Design by Semadar Megged.

THE LIBRARY OF CONGRESS HAS CATALOGED THE PHILOMEL BOOKS EDITION AS FOLLOWS:
Abrahams, Peter, date.
Giving to the poor / Peter Abrahams.
p. cm.—
(Outlaws of Sherwood Street ; 2)
Summary: "Robbie and friends, using a magical charm, protect a Canarsee Indian burial ground from urban developers."—Provided by publisher. [1. Conduct of life—Fiction. 2. Justice—Fiction. 3. Magic—Fiction. 4. Cemeteries—Fiction. 5. Indians of North America—New York (State)—Fiction. 6. Neighborhoods—Fiction. 7. Schools—Fiction. 8. Family life—New York (State)—New York—Fiction. 9. Brooklyn (New York, N.Y.)—Fiction.] I. Title.
PZ7.A1675Rnc 2013 [Fic]—dc23 2012026862
ISBN 978-0-399-25503-8 (hc)

Puffin Books ISBN 978-0-14-751150-8

Printed in the United States of America

1 3 5 7 9 10 8 6 4 2

1

"Sentimental crap," my dad said, poking his head into the living room where Mom and I were watching *A Christmas Carol,* the old black-and-white version. My dad—Chas Forester, in case you're looking for him on the bookstore shelves—is a writer, so his opinion counts when it comes to stories. His first book, *All But the Shouting,* came out my kindergarten year—I'm now in seventh grade—and almost got made into a movie. *On/Off,* his second novel, was over a thousand pages long, a completely amazing accomplishment all by itself, in my opinion, and now he was working on what he called a fictional memoir, which sounded brilliant based just on that, and had already sent in fifty pages to a publisher or maybe an agent, I couldn't remember which.

"Then why are you still watching?" my mom said. My mom's a lawyer, always real quick with the killer question. But it was true. Dad was lingering in the doorway, his eyes fixed on the screen, where Scrooge was leaning out of the window and asking the surprised kid on the snowy street whether the prize goose was still at the poulterer's, my favorite moment in the movie. And were my dad's eyes suddenly a little misty? I turned for a closer look, and he was no longer there.

We weren't the kind of family that made a big deal out of Christmas. Dad screwing together the parts of the flimsy little artificial tree; Mom stocking up on organic eggnog from Ditmas Dairy; *A Christmas Carol* on TV; and Christmas music, mostly Al Green, coming through the speakers—that was about it. Pretty close to a non-event, but this year I was looking forward to it like never before. I needed a break, wanted things to slow down for a while. My Outlaw friend Silas—the other Outlaws being Ashanti and Tut-Tut—had once explained how fast we were really moving—the earth doing a three-sixty every day and also zooming around the sun once a year, and meanwhile our galaxy, the Milky Way, was rotating, too, and at the same time the whole big mess, like a gigantic Frisbee, was flying away from where the big bang happened, meaning we were now, like, ten thousand miles from where we were when Scrooge asked about the goose, and the kid hadn't even run out of the frame yet! Silas was smart—he'd taught himself calculus just so he could make an app for popping open inconvenient combination locks, an app that had worked like a charm when we needed it, actually better in some ways than the real charm we'd had at the time—but all the same, I needed a break.

Scrooge walked off into the sunset with Tiny Tim, who no longer needed his cane, maybe because he was eating better now that Scrooge had doubled his dad's salary.

"Mom?" I said. "We're, like, a million miles from where we were at the start of the movie."

Mom gave me a look. She has dark, watchful eyes, which look best, in my opinion, when they're softening, like now.

"What an interesting thought," she said. "Do you mean in terms of what the movie has taught us about generosity, things like that?"

"Not really," I said. In fact, for the first time in my life, I was edging toward my dad's take on the movie. I explained the whole Milky Way thing, probably not well.

My mom's eyes started unsoftening. "If true," she said, "does it have any actual meaning for us down here?"

I was pretty sure it did, but no way could I argue the case.

"And even if it did," Mom went on, "what could we do about it?"

"Hit the brakes," I said.

Mom laughed, checked her watch. "How does Thai sound?"

"Great."

She handed me some money. "How about taking Pendleton?"

"Sure." Pendleton lay by the artificial tree. "Pendleton?" I said. "Pendleton?"

No response. His eyes remained closed. His tail didn't even twitch. Pendleton didn't like the cold. Nor did he like the heat. Wind bothered him, and also rain. The one time he'd seen hail had turned into a nightmare. I went by myself.

We live in an apartment that takes up the top two floors of an old brownstone in Brooklyn. Mitch, the landlord, lives on the ground floor. I heard him practicing his saxophone, pretty much all he did since losing his Wall Street job right after Thanksgiving. It's a fine building, with good bones, my mom says, on the shady side of the street and halfway up a hill. As you climb the hill, the western view opens up in stages, like you're rising in an elevator: the East River, the Brooklyn Bridge, Manhattan. It was only about six o'clock, but the sky was already dark and the lights of the city glowed and blinked on the water. We'd had a big snowstorm, which, looking back, couldn't have come at a better time, but in the city the snow gets removed as fast as possible—because the mayor's reelection depends on it, my dad says—and what remains quickly turns crusty and black. I crunched over a frozen snowbank full of half-buried things—a beer can, cigarette butts, a glove, poop that hadn't been scooped—turned onto the next block, went past the halfway house for guys with mental problems, all of them inside at the moment, meaning it had to be dinner-time—and came to Your Thai.

Your Thai, the best takeout in all of Brooklyn, was one of those places below street level. I went down the stairs and stepped into a world full of smells from a warmer land. The kitchen part was behind the counter at the back. In front stood a few tables, but there was only one customer, a woman bent over a bowl of soup, her face hidden by her long blond hair; nicely cut hair, I noticed, with subtle golden highlights, and sort of fluffy, like it had just been blow-dried. I'd been on the lookout for highlights lately, planned on raising the subject with my mom as soon as I'd nailed down the exact right shade of vermilion.

Mr. Nok, the owner, was chopping onions—red, yellow, and white—at amazing speed, his knife a silvery blur. He used a huge knife and wore the tallest chef's hat I'd ever seen, but was himself a tiny man, barely coming up to my chin, and I'm maybe a very little bit above average for my age, which happened to be twelve for the time being.

Mr. Nok glanced up and saw me. "Miss Robbie," he said, and gave me a big smile. I didn't like being called that and had told him "just Robbie" a few times, but it hadn't taken.

"Hi, Mr. Nok," I said, moving toward the counter, past the woman with soup. I had the feeling she looked up as I went by, but when I checked, her head was down again. "I'd like some takeout."

"Let me make some guessing," he said. "*Kaeng phet ped yang*?"

My favorite dish in the whole world—although it took me a moment to catch on to Mr. Nok's pronunciation—a kind of red curry with roast duck, the taste indescribable, at least by me.

"Yeah," I said.

Mr. Nok laughed and pumped his fist like he'd just won some big prize. I couldn't help laughing too, even if the knife was still in his hand, making his fist-pump kind of scary if you looked at it in a certain way.

"Plus *tom yum* soup," I said, which my mom loved, "and the grilled shrimp salad with coconut-lime dressing," always my dad's go-to dish from Your Thai.

"Coming up right," said Mr. Nok. He called something toward the back of the kitchen, and Mrs. Nok entered through a beaded curtain—an even smaller figure than Mr. Nok, her long black hair so glossy and alive—and got to work. "In the meanwhile," Mr. Nok said to me, "maybe you would be so kind as helping me write notice in English."

"Sure, Mr. Nok," I said. "What kind of notice?"

He leaned forward, lowered his voice. "You remember when you and your tall friend—"

"Ashanti?"

"Yes, Ashanti—when you were here and things was going not too good?"

"Last month?"

"So hard for understanding," Mr. Nok went on, "American lawsuit problems."

"I heard," I said, and again thought I felt the gaze of the soup-eating woman on my back. I lowered my voice and said in a vague sort of way, "Something about the New Brooklyn Redevelopment Project?" Actually, I probably knew the whole story better than anyone in the world: how the New Brooklyn Redevelopment Project—just a fancy name for the greedy dreams of Sheldon Gunn, who was already one of the richest men in the world—started raising rents all over Brooklyn in order to drive ordinary people out of their homes and businesses so Sheldon Gunn and his people—which sort of included my mom's law firm, Jaggers and Tulkinghorn, although not her, personally, but still a complication—could build gigantic malls and towers for other rich people, and how we, meaning me, Ashanti, Tut-Tut, and Silas had somehow stopped him with the help of a tiny charm, lost at sea in all that wildness at the end, and also without anyone knowing. Not so easy to put in a nutshell.

"Yes, yes, the redevelopment," Mr. Nok was saying. "They wanted big, big pile money from me. And then is come a miracle—someone pushing all the money I was needing and more in here through the mail slot."

"Yeah?" So much fun, that *yeah,* like I was one cool dude.

"But who?" said Mr. Nok. "For this I want to put a notice on wall, to thank the good person."

"Uh," I said, "I'm sure just knowing everything's all right and you're still in business would be enough thanks."

"I do not understand," Mr. Nok said.

I tried again, but he didn't get it.

"It is important to thank the good person," he said, pushing a sheet of paper and a pen my way. "Write, please—thank you, good person. Please eat for free for the rest of your life here at Your Thai. Mr. and Mrs. Nok."

I wrote *To the good person or persons who recently helped us out—you are welcome to eat for free. The Noks.* I read it aloud.

Mr. Nok shook his head. "No Noks," he said. "Mr. and Mrs."

"Okay," I said, and made the change.

"And what about for the rest of the life?"

I added that in.

"Read again, please."

I read it again.

Mr. Nok nodded. "Many thank-yous." He took the notice, walked out from behind the counter, and tacked it up on the wall. At the same time, Mrs. Nok came up to the counter with my bag of takeout.

"On house," said Mr. Nok, handing it to me.

"What?" I said. He knew? "Oh, my God!"

"For writing me the notice," he said.

"Oh, that." For a moment, I'd thought the truth had suddenly dawned on him and I'd hit the free-for-life jackpot, a bad and probably dangerous idea. "Um, I really couldn't, Mr. Nok." I took out the money my mom had given me. He made a pushing-away gesture with his hands.

"Thanks, Mr. Nok," I said, feeling like it was justified this once, since no way I'd ever be claiming that lifetime thing. I took the bag and walked out and, as I did, heard the squeak of a chair and then footsteps behind me. I turned and caught my first clear look at the soup-eating woman's face, which was hard and narrow, the last thing you might expect to be framed by that cheerleader-style hair.

I knew her. No, didn't know her, exactly, since we'd never met, more like I knew who she was, as did maybe hundreds of thousands of other TV watchers. This was

Dina DeNunzio, a reporter for one of the New York stations. I'd also once seen her in person, when I'd been part of the crowd on the street where she'd interviewed Sheldon Gunn about a mysterious fire at one of his properties; although we, the Outlaws, knew it was no mystery to Mr. Gunn.

She followed me up to street level—following, beyond doubt. It felt different from just happening to climb the stairs one after the other. So I wasn't surprised when, at street level, I felt a tap on my shoulder and she said, "Excuse me?"

I stopped and turned. Dina DeNunzio gazed at me through narrowed eyes.

"You look very familiar," she said.

"I'm not," I told her.

"Where do I know you from?"

"Nowhere."

I turned to go. Dina DeNunzio put a hand on my arm, but very gently, a surprise that held me there: me, a streetwise city kid.

2

My name's Dina DeNunzio," she said.

"I know," I told her. "I've seen you on TV."

"And I just can't shake the feeling I've seen you, too," Dina said.

"I've never been on TV."

She laughed. "Doesn't matter," she said. "The point is, Robbie, that—"

"Hey! How do you know my name?"

"Your Thai is such a small place," she said. "I couldn't help overhearing your conversation with the owner"—she took out a notebook—"Nopadon Nok. My apologies if I've offended you." She let go of my arm.

"No, no," I said, not offended, more like uncomfortable. And also a bit distracted: Mr. Nok's first name was Nopadon? Nopadon Nok, all those *n*'s and *o*'s. It was like a tiny poem.

"And I couldn't help but also observe the good

relationship that the two of you seem to have," Dina went on. "Which is why I'm hoping you might be able to help me with a story I'm working on."

"Uh, what story?" I said.

"It's about the New Brooklyn Redevelopment Project," she said.

"I don't know anything about that."

Dina smiled, like I'd just cracked a joke. "My mistake—I could have sworn I heard you and Mr. Nok discussing it."

"Well, I've heard of it," I said. "I am a citizen of Brooklyn."

"Nice," she said. "Can I quote you? I'll need your last name." She took out a pen, flipped to a new page in her notebook.

"Quote me?" Her pen hovered over the page, like a thin creature about to pounce.

"You'd prefer this to be off the record?"

My true preference was for this to be all over right now. How to put that politely?

"No problem," Dina said before an idea had come to me.

She closed the notebook and tucked it away in her jacket, a very cool jacket, I noticed: rich red leather with a thick zipper and matte-finish studs. At that moment, for the first time, an answer to that annoying question kids often get—What do you want to be when you grow up?—hit me: a journalist!

"But," Dina went on, "I'd be interested in what you know about the NBRP."

I shrugged my shoulders. I was wearing my somewhat puffy winter jacket with the white shoulder patches, a jacket I'd loved until a few seconds ago and was now starting to hate.

"Just that they were raising rents and stuff," I said.

"What do you know about Sheldon Gunn?"

"Never heard of him."

"No?" Dina said. "He's quite a prominent figure in New York. Owns *Boffo,* the biggest private yacht in the world. It's often in the news."

"Yeah?" I said. In fact, as I knew from research Ashanti and I had done, *Boffo* was only the second biggest yacht in the world. I also knew what it was like to sneak onboard in the middle of the night on the open sea and soon be facing a grim and violent death. "Never heard of it, either."

"What about that notice—the anonymous benefactor shoving cash through the mail slot?"

"Kind of amazing."

"Are you aware that similar money dumps took place in other parts of Brooklyn that same night?"

I shook my head.

"No idea who the benefactor or benefactors might be?"

"No. This is all news to me."

Dina gave me one of her narrow-eyed looks, then handed me her card. "In case you do hear anything, please keep me in mind."

"Sure," I said. "But why would I be hearing anything?"

"Because you're a kid," Dina said. "And the rumor going around is that a band of kids is mixed up in all this, kind of modern-day Robin Hoods."

A jolt went through me, made my knees go weak and stopped my breathing. My world shrank down to that narrow-eyed look outside and the wild panic inside. "Oh?" I said, my voice quite a bit higher than usual, up there in six-year-old range. I forced myself to breathe again, tried to get my voice back under control. "Really?" Really: the puniest response there was.

"That's the rumor." Did Dina's lips start curving up in that little smile? The nearest streetlight was out, so I couldn't be sure. "But if true, I'd have a sympathetic reaction, if you see what I mean."

"I don't."

"My coverage would be positive," Dina said. "Here's something you might not have realized—shown in the right light, those kids could be stars."

"Huh?"

"Why not? Wasn't Robin Hood a star?"

"Robin Hood wasn't even a real person for sure," I said. "And maybe these . . . kids of yours aren't real either."

Now Dina did smile. "Great answer," she said. "You'd be a terrific interview."

I started shaking my head. She held up her hand.

"Someday," she said. "Maybe. No pressure."

No pressure: I liked hearing that, began to relax a little, which was just when Dina asked one more question.

"And your last name, again?"

"Forester." I just blurted it out, taken by surprise, thrown by that sneaky *again,* too dumb to live.

"Robbie Forester," Dina said. Then came a strange silence, with my name just sort of hanging there between our breath clouds. "What an interesting name."

Things had gotten suddenly busy back home, not unusual. Mom was at her desk, paging impatiently through a long document, her ear to the phone: Mom's job had to do with restructuring debt, about which I had no clue. All I knew was that debt could need restructuring at any hour of the day or night. As for my dad, I could hear him upstairs, pacing around. Pacing around meant he was wrestling with a new idea. Those wrestling matches could also happen at any hour of the day or night.

I called out, "I'm back," then went to the kitchen, got out the chopsticks, opened the Your Thai cartons, and dug in.

Surprise. I turned out not to be hungry. Not hungry even though I hadn't eaten since lunchtime at school and here was fresh and steaming *kaeng phet ped yang* right before my eyes?

But all I could think of was, *What an interesting name.* It closed my stomach up tight.

I went upstairs to my room. From my parents' room down the hall came the sound of my dad, still pacing, plus "but if . . ." and "why couldn't . . ." and "that would mean . . ." and more writer talk like that. I already knew one thing for sure: no way I wanted to be a writer. A reporter, on the other hand? I entered my room, stood in front of the mirror, tried out narrow-eyed looks, some with glasses on and one blurry take with glasses off. Have I mentioned that I wear glasses? And that Dr. Singh, the ophthalmologist, won't even consider contacts until you're thirteen?

I won't bother to describe my room, except to say it's not big. But in the city you're lucky to have a bedroom all to yourself—although the truth is Pendleton is sort of my roommate. For example, at the moment he was lying on the bed, taking up most of the space. Pendleton's a very big, tweedy-looking mix of this and that, and also timid and lazy. His sleepy eyes followed me across the room. He worked up the energy to raise his tail a few inches and let it fall in a soft thump of greeting.

"Move over."

He didn't budge. I squeezed onto a corner of the bed and gave him a pat. "We've got a problem, Pendleton. Any ideas?"

He licked my hand, one of his two or three go-to ideas. I took out my phone, texted Ashanti, got no response, called, and was sent to voice mail. I called Silas.

"Yo," he said.

"Silas? Please don't say yo."

"Why not?"

"It's not you."

"What's me?"

"I don't know," I said. "We need to talk."

"About what's me?"

"Oh, my God. Silas!"

"Yo."

I took a deep breath. Friendship with Silas—if that was indeed what we had—involved taking a lot of deep breaths. "Do you know who Dina DeNunzio is?"

"Spokesman for the pope."

"What are you talking about?"

"That's what a nuncio does. I've read all about the

popes. For a while, there were two at a time, although you probably knew that."

I hadn't known that. Silas was a homeschooler, knew things no one else did. "Dina DeNunzio's a TV reporter. She's been sniffing around."

"Sniffing around what?"

"Think."

"Can't you just tell me? I'm kind of busy right now."

I tried and tried not to say "doing what?" and failed.

"Know those automatic flushing toilets?" he said. "I'm building an app that will flush every single one of them within a three-mile radius at my command."

"Is that a good idea?"

"Can't think of a better one."

"Let's do this in person," I said.

"Do what?"

"Our talk. It's a half day for me and Ashanti tomorrow. Can you be at HQ around noon?"

"I was kind of planning to sleep in."

"Noon, Silas. Be there."

Now's the time, no avoiding it, to admit that I go to private school, namely Thatcher Academy. Not my idea. Some kids from my part of Brooklyn got sent to private school right from kindergarten. Others made the switch later. My parents, on account of their beliefs about society, had waited until what all their friends said was the last possible moment—namely seventh grade, if they had any ambition for me at all—and then caved.

Of course, lots of kids stayed in public school, Tut-Tut for example. Which was why, the next morning, I walked to Thatcher instead of taking the train—twenty-five blocks including the detour to stop by my old public school, Joe Louis, where Tut-Tut went. It was the best way to get in touch with Tut-Tut: he didn't have a phone, didn't have much at all.

I came to the chain-link that enclosed the Joe Louis school yard, a small yard with cracked pavement and litter in the corners, and looked through. Three kids were shooting hoops at the single backboard, but everyone else was clustered around the doors, waiting for the bell to ring and free them from the cold. Tut-Tut could usually be found at a spot of smooth pavement behind the backboard, making his little chalk drawings. Tut-Tut was very artistic, made wonderful drawings, usually of things like parrots or flowers from Haiti, which was where he was from.

I didn't see him. Kind of odd, because Tut-Tut didn't like to hang around his apartment, always got to school early and stayed late. Tut-Tut lived in the projects with his uncle; I'd met the uncle, and understood.

The bell rang. I checked down the street in the direction Tut-Tut would be coming from. No Tut-Tut. The basketball players took their last shots and started shuffling reluctantly toward the school building. They were all boys, two of them already sporting fuzzy mustaches. I picked the unmustached one and called through the fence.

"Where's Tut-Tut?" Toussaint was actually Tut-Tut's real name, but no one used it.

"Huh?" said the kid.

"You know," said one of the others. "That loser."

And the third one said, "Th-th-th-that l-l-l-l-" That—a lame imitation of Tut-Tut's stutter—broke them all up, like it was the highest form of comedy.

"He's not a loser," I said. "Where is he?"

They all came to the fence. "Who are you?" said the one with the thickest mustache.

I gave him a closer look. Carlos something or other: he'd been in the class across the hall the year before, my last year at Joe Louis, but six inches shorter then, and baby-faced.

"Robbie," I said. "I used to be in Ms. Hernandez's class."

He squinted at me. "Yeah?"

"Yeah."

"Where are you now?"

"That doesn't matter. I'm looking for Tut-Tut."

"Why?"

"We're friends."

"Tut-Tut ain't got no friends."

"You're wrong about that."

"Yeah? If you're such a good friend, how come you don't know he's gone?"

"Gone? What do you mean—gone?"

"INS got him," the mustached kid said. "Swept him right up."

"G-g-g-gone," said the mimicker, getting an even bigger laugh this time.

3

Other than Ashanti, I hadn't made many friends at Thatcher. Yet. I had to keep that *yet* in mind. But there were lots of good things about the school, including the beauty of the building itself—a grand nineteenth-century affair on the outside, light and modern on the inside, with all the best of everything. Another good thing, maybe the best, was the fact that there weren't nearly as many actual school days as in public school. Today, for example, and a half day at that, was the end of the semester, and at Joe Louis, they still had almost a week to go.

Half day meant my last class was history with Mr. Stinecki. The male teachers at Thatcher always wore ties. Mr. Stinecki was wearing a tie decorated with martini glasses, one of his favorites. He was in his second year at Thatcher, and the word was it would be his last.

"Here are the robber baron essays," he said, passing them out. The topic: *Robber Barons or Captains of Industry?*

Discuss with reference to a least three people from the following list. . . . And then had come all those names, lots of which you still saw on buildings, even though the men themselves were long dead. Rockefeller, Morgan, Carnegie, Flagler. Signe Stone, who sat next to me, was a Flagler on her mother's side; at the moment, she had her head down, busy texting someone. I couldn't help but notice her grade: A big red A. I myself got a big red B minus. *You've drawn interesting parallels to contemporary circumstances, Robbie, but that wasn't the topic. Also you referenced only two names from the list. Other than that, nice job.* At Joe Louis I'd never had a grade less than A; at Thatcher I still didn't have even one. Three names from the list! How had I slipped up on that?

"Merry Christmas, Happy Hanukkah, Killer Kwanzaa," Mr. Stinecki said, as we all filed out at the end of class. "Anybody know of a vacant ski house, by the way?"

The eighth-graders had their lockers outside the music room, which was where I found Ashanti. "Hey," she said. "Didn't get back to you last night."

"I noticed."

She shot me a quick look. "Don't need any attitude right now."

Ashanti could be very intimidating. She was tall and beautiful, but not at all cute or even pretty. What else? There was how she carried herself, for one thing, head up and confident. Plus her coffee-crème skin, always clear and unblemished, even though the rest of us were living through the age of sneak-attack blemishes that could strike at any time.

"I was just saying I noticed is all," I said. "What am I supposed to do—not notice things I notice?"

Ashanti glared down at me, like some biting remark was on the way, and then came a big surprise: her eyes misted up and she turned quickly away and started rummaging around inside her locker, rummaging like she was annoyed at the things in there.

"What?" I said. "What's going on?"

"Not now."

"But we need to talk."

Now she turned on me, her voice rising. "What the hell about?"

My voice rose, too. "Dina DeNunzio, for one thing," I said. "She—" At that moment, I grew aware of someone passing behind us in the hall and possibly slowing down. I whipped around and there was Mr. Stinecki. He looked away, not meeting my gaze, and sped up.

"What about her?" Ashanti said, taking a book out of her locker and slamming it shut.

"Shh," I said, touching her shoulder. We exchanged a look, hard to describe except to say that maybe it was the kind of look that only people who'd been through big danger together could share. We said no more until we were out on the street.

It was clear and cold outside, the sky an icy blue, the snow on Thatcher's block all removed except for a blackened snowbank or two. We crossed the street, passed an old woman wearing multiple layers with a New York Giants football jersey on top. She paused to fish cans out of a trash barrel. We kept going, and I told Ashanti about Mr. Nok, Dina DeNunzio, Silas, HQ, and—way more important—Tut-Tut.

"Whoa," Ashanti said. "Just because those jerks told you he got busted doesn't mean it's true. They have to say stuff like that to keep up their jerkdom memberships."

"You saying we should pay a visit to Tut-Tut's place?"

"I was just about to," Ashanti said. We hurried to the next subway stop, took the stairs down two at a time, because there was a rush of cold air in our faces,: a train was on its way. We swiped our cards and hopped on just as the doors were closing.

We got off two stops away, ran up to street level. Across the street stood the Quality Coffin Company—"Reliable and Dependable Since 1889." The delivery door was open, and inside I could see a worker loading a coffin onto the back of a truck. He had no trouble handling the coffin by himself: it was a very small coffin.

"Christ," Ashanti said, as though our thoughts were running parallel. Then she added, "When sorrows come, they come not single spies but in battalions."

"What's that?"

"Something we learned in English today. It always happens when you least expect it."

"Sorrow coming?"

She shook her head no. "Something from school suddenly making sense."

"I'm still waiting," I said.

Ashanti laughed.

We went by some auto repair shops, the sidewalks all greasy in front of them. "In that sorrows thing," I said, "were you including whatever you were going to tell me back at school?"

Ashanti gazed into the distance. "Later," she said, and a silence fell between us.

On the next block, we came to Tut-Tut's place, if that was how to put it. Tut-Tut lived in the projects—in this case, on the third floor of a dark brick high-rise wedged in between two high-rises just like it. Someone had spilled a plastic garbage bag full of clothes in the treeless, bushless yard out front, clothes that must have been wet and now were frozen in strange positions that no human could adopt.

We walked to the big front door, a glass door smeared

with many handprints that glared in the sunshine. It was locked.

"Now what?" said Ashanti, who'd never been here before.

"We just wait," I told her.

And in a minute or two, a bony-faced woman in a hoodie came hurrying out. I caught the door before it closed. An old man drinking from a paper-bag-wrapped bottle watched us cross the little lobby to the elevator.

"Dream on," he said.

I pressed the button.

"But it ain't gonna come true," said the old man. "Crappy thing's out of order."

"Then there should be a sign," Ashanti snapped at him.

Ashanti could startle people, even adults sometimes, but not this guy. He laughed, took another swig, and again said, "Dream on."

We took the stairs. The air turned very warm right away, stiflingly hot, actually, and full of smells, none of them good. On the third floor, we walked down a dim hall, where things cooled down again, all the way to cold. Some of the doors had Christmas decorations on them, but not Tut-Tut's. I knocked.

On the other side of the door, a man yelled, "He's got the drop on you," and a woman screamed, "Shoot the sucker." Then came blasts of machine-gun fire, *ACK-ACK-ACK, ACK-ACK-ACK.* I recognized that stupid dialogue from a video game Silas liked to play, *Death Commandos in Hell,* and knocked again, harder. Inside the sound got turned down, footsteps moved across the floor, and a man called, "Who's there?" His English was very good, with just a trace of a Haitian accent, which sounds kind of French. This was Tut-Tut's uncle, Jean-Claude. I smelled booze right through the door.

"Is Tut-Tut here?" I said.

The door opened. Uncle Jean-Claude peered down at us, forty-ouncer in hand. He was tall and thin, and resembled Tut-Tut in some ways—they had the same high cheekbones, for example. But the effect was very different: Tut-Tut's face was sweet, Jean-Claude's mean. Over his shoulder I could see the TV, a futuristic war frozen on the screen.

His bloodshot eyes went to me, then Ashanti, and back. Did he even remember me? He'd been pretty wasted the only time we'd met, a nasty occasion that had ended with Jean-Claude knocking Tut-Tut to the floor with a vicious backhand blow and Tut-Tut and me taking off. Recognition dawned, which I knew from his face getting meaner.

"You," he said.

No denying that. "Is Tut-Tut here?" I said.

He turned and called over his shoulder in a high voice, maybe mimicking me. "Boy! Are you here?"

Silence.

"Don't look like it," Jean-Claude said.

"Do you know where he is?" I said. "He wasn't in school today."

Jean-Claude put his hand over his chest in a dramatic sort of way. "Not in school today? How will he ever get ahead in this earthly life?"

I could feel Ashanti's anger rising. It jumped the space between us, like some kind of instant contagion, and set me off. "What the hell?" I said. "Why are you doing this? Just tell us!"

For a moment, I thought Jean-Claude was about to get angry too. Instead he smiled and said, "Well, well. A hotheaded young chick." He glanced at Ashanti. "Two hotheaded young chicks." And now he did start to look angry, or at least annoyed. "How does that little retard get friends like you?"

"He's not a retard," we said together.

"No?" said Jean-Claude. "Then how come the INS grabbed him?"

"Oh, no!" I said. "Is it true?"

"Couldn't be truer," said Jean-Claude.

"Why didn't they grab you?" Ashanti said.

"I'm no retard," Jean-Claude said. He reached into

his pocket and pulled out a laminated card with his photo on it. "Plus, I have this, and he doesn't."

"What is it?" I said.

"A green card," Jean-Claude said. His chin tilted up. "I'm as legal as you."

I gazed at the green card. It wasn't even green. For some reason, that seemed important to me.

"How did it happen?" Ashanti said.

Jean-Claude shrugged.

"Come on," she said. "There must be illegal immigrants all over the city."

"Yeah," I said. "Why did they pick on Tut-Tut?"

"Don't ask me," Jean-Claude said, but his eyes shifted, not meeting ours.

"Oh, my God!" I said.

"You dimed him out," said Ashanti.

Jean-Claude raised the forty-ouncer, practically poured it down his throat, then wiped his mouth on the back of his sleeve. "Think what you want," he said.

What I wanted was to do something real bad to him. All I could think of was grabbing that green card, held loosely in his non-beer hand, so that was what I did.

Jean-Claude called me a name I'm not going to repeat and tried to snatch it back, but he was slow and clumsy, maybe much drunker than I'd thought. I retreated into the hall, Ashanti right beside me. He took a step or two after us, his movements unsteady.

"Where is he?" Ashanti said.

"Tell us, and you get it back," I said.

He called me that name again, then tried out another ugly one on Ashanti. We just stood there, not saying a word. It wasn't that we were being brave—at least in my case—more just that I was so worried and confused about Tut-Tut that I forgot to be afraid.

"All right, have it your way," Jean-Claude said. He held out his hand. "First the card."

I shook my head. "First the information," said Ashanti.

Jean-Claude thought for a moment or two, then nodded. "Sure," he said, "for what good it will do you. They've got him down at the Flatbush Family Detention Center."

"But that's like a jail," Ashanti said.

"Like?" said Jean-Claude. "Couldn't be liker."

I tossed him the card, an accurate toss that he failed to catch. He bent to pick it up, and we were out of there.

4

We walked away from the projects and went left at the next cross street. The sign, hanging crookedly from a single bolt, read Sherwood Street. Sherwood Street was a strange street, only a single block long, and populated by no one. On the far side stood an abandoned gas station and a fenced-in scrap metal foundry that never seemed to be open; on our side were an empty and weedy trash-strewn lot and then a huge boarded-up warehouse. Ashanti and I turned into the alley that ran along the side of the warehouse and walked to the back.

We glanced around, saw we were alone, and climbed up on the loading dock. The entrance to the warehouse was a big roll-down steel door, padlocked at the bottom, but set in the big steel door was a small door for people to use when they weren't loading or unloading. The small door no longer had a knob—a metal plate covered the hole where the knob had been—and a piece of plywood covered the window space. The first time Tut-Tut had brought me here, he'd pried the plywood off with a butter knife. Now Silas had it rigged so all you had to do was point your cell phone and press 13. Why 13? That was Silas.

I pointed my phone and pressed 13. The plywood cover swung open. Ashanti reached through the glassless space, opened the door from the inside. We entered, the plywood closing back in place automatically. Behind us a deep male voice said, "Welcome to the Casbah." I'd freaked the first time that had happened, but it was just a sound clip from some old movie Silas had found.

It was dim inside the warehouse—just a few narrow blades of light leaking in from places where the boarding up had been a little careless—but we knew our way. We moved along a row of tall floor-to-ceiling pillars to the lift at the far side of the warehouse, a square steel slab with no doors or windows. We stepped on the slab and pressed a button on the wall, a button Tut-Tut had painted with his purple tag in tiny form: *vudu*. The steel slab shuddered and slowly rose through an opening in the ceiling.

At the floor level above, we came to a stop. We were in a small room with a desk, some office-type swivel chairs, and Tut-Tut's spray paintings on the wall: parrots, flowers, butterflies, and the *vudu* tag again, much bigger, plus portraits of Tut-Tut, his dead parents (their eyes were closed), Jean-Claude, and all of us as a group—me, Ashanti, Silas, Tut-Tut. This was HQ, the secret place Tut-Tut had found, exactly how he'd never explained. His stutter made explaining things hard, especially long, complicated stories, and he ended up getting impatient with himself. Normally we'd have had to switch on the light—a single bulb hanging from the ceiling—but it was already on and Silas was sitting at the desk, eating fast-food fries.

"My mistake, amigos," he said. "I assumed you meant noon eastern time."

"You've got ketchup all over your face," Ashanti said.

Silas stuck out his tongue at a weird sideways angle, kind of like Pendleton, and licked ketchup off his cheek. It was a roundish sort of cheek, and Silas was a roundish sort of kid, red-haired with freckles and green eyes that took in everything. He had one of those very expressive faces, like an actor. Right now it was expressing self-satisfaction, maybe because he'd pulled the space heater right up beside him and was hogging all the heat.

"Planning on sharing those fries?" I said.

"Be my guest," said Silas. "Although I should warn you I feel a cold coming on."

I left the fries alone, but not Ashanti, who grabbed the container and dug right in. Silas frowned at her.

"What's your problem?" she said, or something like that. Hard to tell with her mouth so full.

Silas shrugged. "Eat and be merry," he said.

But we weren't feeling merry, me and Ashanti, and neither was Silas after we told him all the news.

"Whoa," he said. "Incoming! Incoming!" And he put his hands over his head.

"Silas?" I said. "What are you doing?"

"You dweeb," said Ashanti.

"I'm not a dweeb," Silas said. "Not by any kind of strict definition."

"A geek?" said Ashanti.

Silas looked offended. "A geek," he said, "is a drunk who bites the heads off live chickens."

Ashanti stopped eating, put the fries on the desk.

"I'm more like a nerd," Silas said, helping himself to another handful, "if you really have to put a label on people."

"Sorry," Ashanti said; kind of a surprise: had I ever heard her say sorry to anybody?

But of course Silas had to blow it. "Apology graciously accepted," he said.

"Jerk," Ashanti said.

"Guys?" I said. Meaning *enough.* They both turned to me. "What are we going to do?" I said.

"If only we still had the charm," Silas said.

"If only won't get it done," Ashanti said.

"I'm not sure it would do any good," I told them.

"Huh?" they said.

"I mean—did we have the charm or did it have us?"

They thought about that. Then Silas said, "I still wish we had it. Maybe we could learn to scuba dive."

"And search where?" Ashanti said.

"The bottom of the sea," said Silas.

"But exactly where? All we know is we were out there somewhere."

Ashanti was right about that. I could see it all, but not in the way you picture things that happened in real life, more the way you picture things that happened in a dream. One of those falling dreams in this case, falling off the helicopter deck of *Boffo,* falling and falling through the night and blowing snow, leveling out at the last moment, so close to death that my arm went plunging into the wild and icy waters, which was when I must have lost the leather bracelet with that strange silver heart.

"Maybe you're right," Silas said. He had some sort of thought that made him frown. "Do you think the scuba diving people expect you to know how to swim?"

"You don't know how to swim?" I said.

"It never came up."

"You've never been to the beach?" Ashanti said.

"I don't like the beach. I burn right away." Silas stuck out his chin. "And what's wrong with indoors? Indoors is a great human invention."

Uh-oh. Great human inventions was one of Silas's favorite topics. This wasn't the time.

"Later, Silas," I said. "What are we going to do? That's the point."

"Simple," he said. "We prioritize."

"Meaning?" I said.

"Meaning start with the most—"

"We know what prioritize means," Ashanti said.

"Then we're all on the same page," said Silas. "But are we in the same paragraph?" He laughed. We didn't join in. That didn't stop him. Finally he wiped away one of those laughter tears and said, "Bottom line, we have all these problems. Priority question—which one is the most important?"

"Tut-Tut," I said.

"Prize for the little lady," said Silas.

"Silas?" said Ashanti, in a way she had—not necessarily loud but plenty forceful—of commanding everyone's attention.

"Oops," said Silas.

"We have to get Tut-Tut out of there," I said.

"Spring him," Silas said.

"Spring him?" said Ashanti.

"That's the expression for busting dudes out of jail," Silas explained.

"But how?" I said.

We sat in silence. I gazed at Tut-Tut's spray-painted self-portrait on the wall. He seemed to be gazing right back at me. There was so much inside him, including lots of pain he'd suffered, although he didn't want anybody's sympathy; I thought I could see all that in the picture.

Silas snapped his fingers. Not one of his talents: he tried it a few more times, barely making a sound. "Anyway," he said, giving up, "I've got it. We'll make him a green card."

"How?"

"Nothing to it," Silas said. "There's a bunch of good programs for that kind of thing. All we need is some green paper and—"

"Green cards aren't green," I said.

"No?"

"And even if we had a green card, how do we get it to him?" I said.

"And even if we get it to him, then what?" says Ashanti. "He flashes it to a guard or something and the doors open, just like that?"

"Why not?" said Silas.

I didn't know the answer, but I did know that in the adult world, doors never seemed to open just like that.

We did more sitting in silence. The getting-nowhere feeling pressed down on me like a heavy cloud. *Do something, Robbie!* That was a voice inside me I sometimes heard, my own voice, often inclined to panic: the voice I thought of as the innermost Robbie.

I rose. "Let's go take a look at the Flatbush Family Detention Center."

"Sounds like a plan," Ashanti said.

"We're going outside?" said Silas.

We gave him a look. He got ready, meaning he buttoned up his cardigan—I'd never seen another human being in a cardigan—wrapped a scarf around his neck, struggled into his Michelin-Man-type jacket, and pulled on an Arctic-explorer-type hat with fur flaps and a pair of mittens. Yes, mittens.

The Flatbush Family Detention Center wasn't actually on Flatbush Avenue, the most important street in the borough, but a few blocks north, so we had to walk from the subway station, a slow walk, on account of a wind springing up right in our faces and the fact of Silas being too bundled up to move well. We passed a few old office low-rises and a fire station, and came to a massive brick building on a corner. It looked something like a school except that the windows were barred, the brick walls were grimier than any school walls I'd ever seen, and two cops stood by the front door. There was no sign out front.

"This is it," Ashanti said.

The cops looked at us. We looked at them.

"Help you kids?" one of them said.

Ashanti stepped forward. "We've got a friend in there."

"Yeah?" said the other cop.

"Yeah," said Ashanti.

I stepped forward too, at the same time sensing Silas backing away. "We want to see him."

"Gotta make arrangements," the second cop said.

"How?" I said.

"Go online," said the first cop. "Click on visitation."

"Okay," said Silas, behind us. "Thanks."

We walked away, not in the direction we'd come from; I had some vague feeling about going around the corner, checking out the rest of the building.

Behind me, Ashanti said, "You came close to saying 'thanks, officer,' didn't you?"

"No way," Silas said. "Plus, how I said thanks was loaded with contempt."

"Right," Ashanti said. "They're probably discussing whether or not to cuff you."

Silas whipped around, looked back.

We turned the corner, kept going, the grimy wall looming above us. Halfway down the block, we came to an archway in the wall, maybe once an entrance for deliveries. The opening was barred now by crisscrossing black metal bars so close together you probably couldn't have squeezed your head through. Beyond the bars, at the far end of the covered barrel space of the arch, were more crisscrossing bars in the same arrangement, and beyond those bars lay a small and treeless paved yard, no one in it. At least no one in the part I could see, almost like a narrow stage framed by the sides of the archway.

"Come on," Silas said. "I'm freezing."

I ignored him, but glanced over at Ashanti. She was stamping her feet, maybe feeling the cold, too. For some reason, I did not.

"Anyone carrying green?" Silas said. "Hot chocolate would go down real nice. With a marshmallow on top."

At that moment, from offstage, if that's how to put it, a rock or maybe a chunk of broken pavement came bouncing across the yard. Then a small figure in a hoodie that was much too big for him came into view and gave the rock a kick. He moved after it, not looking at us: a small figure in a too-big hoodie, torn jeans—nothing hip or cool about those tears—and my old white sneakers with the blue trim, both of them now laceless. And no socks, despite the cold. That—the no socks part—bothered me more than anything, kind of crazy. I called his name.

"Tut-Tut."

5

Tut-Tut turned quickly, and the look on his face—or more accurately the way it changed, from deep inward sadness and worry to pure joy—was something I know I'll never forget. He ran to the inner barrier, grabbed the bars and said, "R-r-r-r-r-." Words starting with *R* were extra hard for Tut-Tut, even in those rare periods when his speech came a little more easily. Not counting the times when the silver heart had worked its magic: then I'd heard him really speak. The very first word he'd uttered, maybe in his whole life, was *ow*.

We all pressed up against the outer barrier, meaning Tut-Tut was about ten or fifteen feet away.

"Tut-Tut," Ashanti said, "how are you?"

I could see how he was: too skinny, those cheekbones too prominent now, plus his dreads seemed limp and lifeless and even dirty—and maybe worst of all—his lip was split.

"G—," he said, "g-g-g-g-g-g-g—"

But of course he was just about the furthest thing from good.

"Hey," Silas said, "what happened to your lip?"

Tut-Tut's face darkened, but only for a moment and then he shook it off, looking happy again. "N-n-n-n-n-n-n-no-noth-th-th-th-th-," he said. "I-I-I-I'm o-o-k-k-k-k-k—"

"What's going on in this place, Tut-Tut?" I said. "Is anyone helping you?"

"N-n-n-n-n—"

"But they must tell you something," I said, "like about what's happening—you know, the, um . . ."

"Procedures," Silas said.

"Yeah," I said. "There must be some kind of procedures." That was one thing I'd learned: the adult world had procedures for just about everything. And here's another: some people, like Sheldon Gunn, for example, were way better than others at making the whole procedure thing work for them.

"P-p-p-p-pr-pr-pr-," Tut-Tut said. Then he made his hand into a gun and shot some imaginary thing in the air, most likely the whole concept of procedures. I laughed, even though there was nothing funny about this situation, the exact opposite. And when I laughed, Tut-Tut smiled—wincing a bit on account of his split lip—and then he stuck his hand, sort of grayish from the cold, through one of the small squares formed by the crisscrossing bars, and gave a little wave. Meanwhile his split lip had opened up and blood was oozing out; he didn't seem to notice.

"We've got to get you out," Ashanti said.

"H-h-h-h-h-," said Tut-Tut. His stuttering had never been so bad.

How. That was the question all right. Then an idea hit me, kind of late arriving considering my mom's job. "Have you got a lawyer?" I said.

He shook his head.

"But you must have a lawyer," I said.

Tut-Tut made the gesture for money, rubbing his thumb and index finger together.

"They have to give you a lawyer," I said, turning to the others. "Don't they? It's on all the cop shows."

"We don't have a TV," Silas said. "Didn't I ever mention that?"

"But you must know about Miranda," Ashanti said.

"Who's she?" said Silas.

The flip side of Silas knowing stuff no one else did was that he didn't know stuff that was common knowledge and took no effort to learn, like celebrity divorce news, for example.

"Miranda rights," Ashanti said. "Or maybe it was the Gideon case. We took this in class, but Mr. Stinecki had a bad cold that day and no one could understand him. The point is that criminals have the right to a lawyer even if they can't pay."

"Tut-Tut's not a criminal," I said.

Tut-Tut shook his head vigorously. He was no criminal. So what was he doing behind bars?

"Tut-Tut," I said, "I'm going to talk to my mom—I'm sure she'll know the right kind of lawyer." Somewhere out of sight a loud buzzer went off. Tut-Tut glanced to the side in the direction the sound had come from.

"G-g-g-g-g . . ." What was it going to be? Got to go? Good-bye? I didn't know. Tut-Tut tried and tried to get it out, and then gave up and did something I'd never seen him do before, namely pound his fist into his open hand, totally frustrated.

From somewhere in the yard came a man's yell. "Hey! Don't hear so good? Move!"

Tut-Tut turned to go.

"Wait," Ashanti said. "Silas—those stupid mittens—toss them to Tut-Tut."

"My mittens?"

"You can get new ones."

"But—"

Ashanti grabbed the mittens right off Silas's hands, folded one into the other, made a sort of ball. This wasn't going to be easy, but Ashanti pretty much made it look that way. She stuck her arm through one of the barred squares and backhanded the mitten ball right through a square on the other side. Tut-Tut caught it.

"Th-th-th-th-th—"

"I have to say it once more, you ain't gonna like it," the unseen man called.

Tut-Tut gave us another tiny wave, and then he was gone. Silas stuffed his bare hands deep into his pockets.

We got off the train, climbed up to street level, Silas headed one way, me and Ashanti in another. As we parted, Silas said, "You guys thinking what I'm thinking?"

"If it's about your mittens, I'm going to smack you," Ashanti said.

Silas stepped back. "I was thinking—what's the melting temperature for those metal bars? Tut-Tut's pretty small—we'd probably only have to melt through one or two."

"Sounds interesting," I said.

"It does?" said Ashanti.

But Silas looked pleased. The lawyer idea was plan A, but how could it hurt to have a backup?

Ashanti and I walked home. We actually live on the same block, practically across the street from each other. Ashanti's mom was maybe the most beautiful woman I'd ever seen; she'd been a model but had now aged out of the modeling business and didn't seem to go out much. Her dad was a film editor who traveled a lot; I still hadn't met him.

We came to Monsieur Señor's, this coffee place where my dad often wrote when he got sick of being home alone. I didn't see him in there now, but Monsieur Señor's had these little chocolate mint squares I loved.

"Wanna grab something to eat?" I said.

"I'm not hungry."

I glanced over at Ashanti. Her eyes had a faraway look.

"You ready to tell me whatever it is you're not telling me?" I said.

"You're so damn persistent," she said. "If you must know—"

"Hey! I don't need to know—"

"I think my dad's . . . seeing someone."

"Seeing someone?" I said. "What does that mean?"

"Come on! Seeing someone, for God's sake," Ashanti said, her voice rising in real fury. "Do I have to spell it out? Another woman."

"He's having an affair?"

"What a stupid expression!" Ashanti said.

I started getting angry, too. "That's not my fault—I didn't make it up. It's the expression."

Ashanti glared down at me. Then her face changed completely, and she actually started to laugh. "What is it about you?" she said.

"Huh?"

She shook her head, made a fist, tapped me lightly on the shoulder. "Thatcha," she said.

I tapped her back. "Comin' atcha," I said. That was a school-spirity thing we did at Thatcher, always with an ironic undertone, very Thatcherite, as I was learning fast.

Ashanti took a deep breath, let it out slowly in a round breath cloud that rose like a balloon. "Maybe it's not true," she said. "But I can't think of another explanation."

"For what?"

"This text I saw on his phone."

"You were snooping on his phone?"

"Hell, no. But he left it in the bathroom, right by the sink, and it beeped while I was brushing my teeth, practically right in my face. And the message was, quote, miss u so much!!! Three exclamation marks."

I thought that over, hoping to come up with some harmless explanation, like . . . but I couldn't. So why did I then hear myself saying, "I'm sure there's a harmless explanation."

"Like?"

"I'll think of one," I said.

"When you do, let me know." Ashanti turned and climbed up the stairs to her front door, moving much slower and heavier than normal. I went home.

At this hour, mid-afternoon on a weekday, you might find my dad at home, in the office, gazing at the screen or rearranging Post-it Notes on his storyboard wall or in the kitchen taking a coffee break, but you'd never find my mom. Associates in big Manhattan law firms like Jaggers and Tulkinghorn worked long hours. My mom hardly ever got home before seven and usually put in another hour or two after dinner. So seeing them both at the kitchen table was a surprise.

They turned to me as I came in. Then came another surprise: my mom had been crying. Uh-oh. My very first thought? My dad was having an affair. Which was impossible. That wasn't my dad, and besides, my parents loved each other a lot. I was surer of that than just about anything in my whole life, so sure I didn't even question why I was so sure.

"Mom? Dad? Is something wrong?"

They looked at each other, then back at me. Both my parents are young looking for their ages—forty-one for my mom, thirty-nine for my dad—but especially my dad, with his unlined face and thick hair, scruffy like a hipster college kid and untouched by gray. All of a sudden and for no reason, I found myself wishing he looked older, a totally whacked-out thought.

"I guess we should tell her," my dad said.

"What?" I said. "Tell me what?" Had someone died, someone closer to my mom than my dad? Nonna! Nonna was my grandmother on my mom's side, lived in Arizona, played golf every day and also went to Zumba and Pilates classes, and hadn't even been sick, at least not that I'd known, but car accidents happened, and Nonna always drove too fast, and—

My mom licked her lips. "I," she began, then started again. "I've been let go."

Let go? Was that the gentler way of saying . . . "Fired?" I said. And regretted it immediately. How harsh it must have sounded, completely unintended: all I'd been trying to do was get an exact grip on what being let go meant.

My mom's eyes filled with tears, but they didn't spill out, and she made no crying sound, which I sensed was all about appearing strong in front of me, a major act of will on her part, even heroic. "Yes," she said. "Fired."

"But how can they do that, Mom?" I remembered something about how well her last review had gone. "You're so great at your job, and you work so hard." I actually threw in a forbidden adjective between *so* and *hard,* but they didn't seem to catch it.

"You're damn right," my dad said.

"Chas," my mom said, "I already told you—none of that factors in. They got rid of thirty-five associates today, as well as forty-two paralegals and support staff, plus five partners, which is practically unheard of."

"But why, Mom? Is it the economy?" I would have had trouble defining economy in good Thatcherite style. Summing up my knowledge, the economy was bad, had been bad for a long time, and angry people were always arguing about it on the channels I didn't watch.

"Partly the economy, yes," my mom said. "Revenues are way down."

"Revenues?"

"The money coming into the firm from work we—from the work done."

Less revenue meant you fired people? Out of the blue came the kind of thought I never had, namely the logical solution to a big problem. "Instead of firing people, why don't all the lawyers just take less pay till things get better?"

"Exactly!" my dad said. "Right on the nail! And here's the answer to your question, Robbie, in five letters—*G-R-E-E-D*."

My mom held up her hand. "Pointless to get into all that. It won't help. And it's even possible that something of that nature could have happened, but not after the Sheldon Gunn fiasco."

My heart went from beating away like normal, meaning I was unaware of it, to a pounding in my chest that couldn't be ignored. "Sheldon Gunn fiasco?" I said.

"I'm sure I mentioned it," my mom said. "The day after the snowstorm, when the New Brooklyn Redevelopment Project deal fell apart, he fired us—and he was one of our biggest clients, worth millions to the firm every year."

"I never understood why it fell apart in the first place," my dad said.

But I sure did.

"It was the financing," my mom said. "His Saudi partners backed out."

"Why?"

"Something to do with our—Christ, I'll have to stop saying that—with the Jaggers and Tulkinghorn capital formation department and Egil Borg's people, but I don't really know. I never worked on any of it."

Egil Borg: a nasty and dangerous man I'd never wanted to think of again. I went over and hugged my mom. "It's so unfair. You had nothing to do with it."

"Collateral damage," my mom said. A few tears did come after that, my mom's and mine, too. My dad got up and patted our backs.

6

"Don't worry," my dad said. "Everything's going to be just fine."

"Of course it is," my mom said, breaking up our little group hug. "I'll just go and change into something"—she raised her arms in a funny way, like she didn't know how she'd come to be dressed how she was, in one of her charcoal-gray work suits—"more comfortable." She went upstairs.

I looked at my dad. He looked at me.

"Your mom's a star, Robbie," he said. "She'll find something in no time."

"Something like what, Dad?"

"Another law firm, of course. There must be more law firms in New York than in any other city in the world."

"But do they all handle that debt stuff mom does?" I said.

"Good question," my dad said. "I'm sure lots of them

must. New York's the center of finance, too, and debt's all part of that."

"What does Mom do?" I said. "I mean exactly."

"Exactly?" my dad said. "It's all about structuring debt."

"Structuring? I thought it was restructuring. Which is it?"

"That's another good question," my dad said. "But the point is it's highly specialized, and it couldn't be clearer that highly specialized is the way to go in this particular zeitgeist."

Zeitgeist? What the heck was that? For some reason, totally unfair, I was starting to feel annoyed at my dad. He was only trying to stop me from worrying, so it couldn't have been his fault that worry was suddenly growing inside me like a real thing, taking up all the air.

"Who knows?" he said. "She might even find something better. The culture at Jaggers left a lot to be desired."

"What do you mean, Dad?"

"The way they treat people," my dad said, and he was about to say more, but at that moment my mom came downstairs, now wearing jeans and the college sweatshirt she'd brought back from her last reunion; she loved the purple cow on the front, although it couldn't have been dorkier in my opinion.

"What are you guys talking about?" she said. She'd

removed the little bit of makeup she wore for work, now looked kind of pale.

"I was just telling Robbie that we're all right, and we'll be all right," my dad said.

My mom nodded but didn't add anything to that.

"Dad says you'll find something else in no time," I said.

"Does he?" she said, and gave my dad a quick, sharp look.

My dad ran a hand through his hair, this gesture he has when he's feeling uncomfortable. "Just making the point that you're so talented, Jane, so good at what you do."

"A lot of talented people got the ax today," my mom said. She turned to me. "But, yes, I've got tons of contacts, and there's that headhunter who's always calling—I'll get started first thing."

Axes? Headhunters? It all sounded so violent and primitive. "Do we have, like, savings?" I said.

"Savings?" my dad said. "Sure we do."

"To a point," my mom said. "There's no immediate danger. And don't forget my severance pay."

No immediate danger? For some reason that sounded very dangerous. What was that quote of Ashanti's? When sorrows come, they come not single something or other but in something or other else? Was it true of all bad things? Suddenly I thought of Tut-Tut, locked up in that horrible place. I had it easy compared to him. Get a grip, Robbie. But as for my plan—persuading my mom to find a lawyer for Tut-Tut—this didn't seem like the right time.

My dad rubbed his hands together, like he was trying to warm things up. "Tell you what," he said. "Let's hit Local for an early dinner."

"Is that what we should be doing now?" my mom said.

"More than ever," said my dad. "We live our normal lives. Why not?" He went over to her, took her in his arms, and gave her a kiss that was—how should I put this?—on the passionate side. What kid wants to see her parents like that? Not this one. And maybe the timing was off for my mom, too, because she kind of pushed him away.

"I was thinking I'd just warm up that lamb stew," my mom said.

"Leftovers?" said my dad. "Come on—it'll be my treat. I got a royalty check today."

"You did?" my mom said.

"What's a royalty check?" I said.

"Profit on book sales," my dad said. "Sheer beautiful profit."

"Is it for *On/Off*?" my mom said, *On/Off* being my dad's most recent book, two or three years old now, the thousand-page one I'd once heard him call "more of an experiment than anything else."

My dad frowned. "*All But the Shouting,*" he said, that being the first book, even older, which had to be good news, money coming in after all this time.

So we went to Local and had an early dinner. Local was the cool neighborhood bar at the moment, serving Uruguayan-inspired tapas. I think I had something made from small birds, but might have misunderstood the waiter. It was delicious. We had a fun time, although conversation died away at the end a bit, Mom getting a faraway look in her eye. Later, on my way to bed, I happened to glance into the office, and on the desk I spotted what looked like a check. Next thing I knew I was at the desk, sort of hovering very lightly, like I wasn't really there. Yes, my dad's check, sheer beautiful profit. In the memo line place at the bottom left corner of the check it read *All But the Shouting, annual royalties.* The amount was $42.78.

The next day, a Saturday, we went to my Uncle Joe's, something we did once a year, always around Christmas. Uncle Joe, my dad's older brother—only by two years, but much older-looking, almost like he could have been my dad's dad—was a surgeon and lived in Saddle Brook (which my dad called Saddle Poop), New Jersey. Like lots of New Yorkers, we didn't own a car, which meant renting one.

"Just a little econobox will do," my mom told my dad as he left for the car rental agency.

Half an hour later came a *beep-beep* from the street, sort of cheerful sounding, if honking could ever be cheerful. We looked out the window, and there was Dad at the wheel of an enormous SUV. I glanced at my mom. She had dark patches under her eyes, like she'd had a bad sleep; the eyes themselves looked very annoyed.

"Welcome to the 'burbs," said my dad, as we drove down Uncle Joe's street. He and Aunt Jenna lived on a cul-de-sac lined with big, beautiful houses spaced far apart. The 'burbs seemed to have more snow than we did in the city, and it was still white and puffy. We turned into Uncle Joe's circular drive. He was out front, wrapping a bright red scarf around the neck of a small snowman.

"It's like living in a damn calendar," my dad said.

Uncle Joe came over as we rolled up. "Hi, everybody!" he said. "Welcome to America."

I laughed and so did my mom. My dad said ha-ha, kind of under his breath. We got out of the car. Uncle Joe gave Dad a hug, Mom a kiss, and me a big smile and a high five. "How are you doing, Robbie?" he said.

"Great."

"No more headaches?"

"Nope."

"Good news," said Uncle Joe.

Back when the charm had first come to me, I'd had some headaches and ended up at Uncle Joe's hospital where tests had shown nothing wrong. Later I'd realized that those headaches had been all about me and the charm getting to know each other, but at the time, I'd been pretty scared. As for not mentioning the charm at the time, I really hadn't yet believed in it, and also hadn't wanted to sound crazy; soon after that, it had been too late. And now it was pointless, since there was no charm, almost as though I'd imagined the whole thing. But Dina DeNunzio, Sheldon Gunn dropping Jaggers and Tulkinghorn, Jaggers and Tulkinghorn dropping my mom: all real.

My mom leaned into the car. "Pendleton? Let's go."

But he was already out of the car, not like him at all to be up and doing so fast. We glanced around and spotted him over by the snowman, just as . . . was he about to . . . ? Yes, he was. Pendleton lifted his leg against the snowman and spread a surprisingly large amount of yellow over that round white body.

We all laughed, especially my dad.

Inside, Aunt Jenna—who'd been a nurse but no longer worked—was busy in the kitchen. "What's cookin'?" Uncle Joe said.

"How does duck sound?" she said.

"Quack quack," said Uncle Joe.

She threw a potato at him. He caught it, pretended it was too hot to handle, then stuck it in his pocket.

"Don't mind Joe," Aunt Jenna said. "He's regressing."

"Let's drink to that," said Uncle Joe. "Champagne, anybody?"

Uncle Joe, Aunt Jenna, and my dad had champagne. I had cider. My mom just wanted water. Uncle Joe shot her a quick glance as he handed her the glass.

"Is Eli home?" I said. Eli was my cousin, now in college.

"He's skiing this Christmas," Aunt Jenna said. "Eight or ten of them are crowding into someone's condo in Stowe."

Everything I heard about college was like that. Sometimes I could hardly wait.

My dad and Uncle Joe went downstairs to shoot pool. My mom slipped into the dining room and checked her phone. Aunt Jenna took a big bag out of the fridge.

"Like oysters, Robbie?"

"Yeah."

"Know how to shuck 'em?"

"No."

"I'll teach you."

Aunt Jenna spread some newspaper on the granite-topped island, dumped oysters out of the bag, took a pair of shucking knives out of a drawer, and gave me one.

She laid an oyster on the newspaper, the rounded side down. "See right here?" she said. "That's the hinge. Move a tiny way like this and then wiggle in the point, give a firm push and—viola, as a friend of mine used to say." The oyster opened right up. "Now you just slice through this thick knob and plop the oyster back in the rounded part for serving. Want to try?"

"Sure."

I tried. It had looked so easy when Aunt Jenna did it, but I couldn't even wiggle in the point. Aunt Jenna didn't say anything, didn't even watch me, just kept shucking steadily away. Then, just as I was about to give up—

"Viola!"

"There you go," Aunt Jenna said. "House rule—you always eat your first oyster." She cut a lemon in half and squeezed some juice on my oyster.

I slurped it down. "These are great."

"Aren't they?" said Aunt Jenna. "And they're local. We're finally cleaning up some of these waters. Up for doing some more?"

"Yeah!"

"I'll leave you to it," Aunt Jenna said. She washed her hands, then went into the dining room.

I picked out another oyster—bigger than the first, with a nice shape and a pearly sort of sheen—and got to work. At the same time, I could hear my mom and Aunt

Jenna talking in low voices, too low for me to catch the words. But my mom's anxiety, and her determination to cover it up, were clear.

I wiggled the curved end of the shucking knife into the oyster's hinge, gave a firm push, adjusting the angle as I did. The knife slid in just right. At the same time, I heard Aunt Jenna saying something about helping out, and my mom raising her voice: "Oh, no, never."

I worked the flat of the knife along the shell, separating the two halves, concentrating my hardest on the small world of this single oyster. Next step: cutting that little knob attachment thing. I bent forward to do that and, at the same moment, saw something shiny lying right on top of the oyster's glistening body. It was a tiny silver heart: the charm.

7

But how could this be? Maybe I was feverish, imagining the whole thing. I felt my forehead. Cool as a cucumber, as they said, although why I wasn't sure: once you took the cucumber out of the fridge, didn't it warm up to room temperature? I closed my eyes, counted silently to three, and opened them. The tiny silver heart was still there, lying on the oyster. Was it possibly some other silver heart, just a normal everyday charm that had fallen off some boater's bracelet and sunk down into an oyster bed? I stuck out my finger, extended it closer and closer toward the silver heart.

SNAP! The oyster closed so fast the motion was just a blur, the sharp edge of the shell slicing into my fingertip. From the oyster came a faint sizzling sound, and a tiny puff of steam rose and dissipated in the air; I caught a faint smell of the sea. The oyster now looked like all the other oysters on Aunt Jenna's granite island, as though it had never been opened. Meanwhile, my finger was bleeding. I stuck it in my mouth, which happened to be the very moment that Aunt Jenna came back into the kitchen.

"Don't tell me," Aunt Jenna said. "You cut your finger."

I took my finger out of my mouth, put my hand in my pocket. "It's just a scratch," I said.

"Let's see," she said.

I showed her. She made me wash it off, then took a Band-Aid from a drawer and wrapped it on my fingertip in one easy, nurse-like motion.

"Thanks," I said. "And I'm getting the hang of it, really."

"Of course you are," said Aunt Jenna. She opened the fridge and took out a serving dish with about two dozen already shucked oysters on it, and added the three or four she'd done while teaching me. "This should do," she said, and with that started gathering all the closed oysters and returning them to the bag.

"Hey," I said, "I'll do that."

"Not a problem," said Aunt Jenna. "I've got 'em." She dropped all the oysters into the bag and placed it in the fridge. "All set," she called, and a minute or two later, we were all seated around the dining room table.

Uncle Joe raised his glass. "To family," he said.

"To family," said everyone, although if my dad joined

in, it wasn't very loudly. I knew that didn't mean my dad didn't care about family; was it something about toasting the whole subject not being cool? I couldn't take it farther than that.

"I'll clear," I said, rising the moment everyone had finished their seconds of Aunt Jenna's homemade pecan pie—the crust perfect, the filling so nutty and not too sweet. "You guys all sit tight." And I carted off the dishes, closing the door to the kitchen behind me with my foot.

"What a kid!" I heard Uncle Joe say.

"We can never get Eli to lift a finger," said Aunt Jenna.

"This is uncharacteristic," my dad said.

I got busy at the dishwasher, made some clattering noise, then raced over to the fridge practically on tiptoe, like some cartoon character, and opened the door. Aunt Jenna's fridge was enormous—two or three of ours would have fit inside—and packed with food, even though there were just the two of them now. I rooted around, searching for that oyster bag, which was one of those normal fish store bags, extra thick and decorated with pictures of lobsters and leaping marlins.

There it was, behind a jug of what looked like fresh-squeezed grapefruit juice. I tugged the bag to the front of the shelf and peered inside: a dozen or so oysters were jumbled together in the bag, none of them in any obvious way different from any of the others. How was that possible? Hadn't my special oyster been quite a bit bigger and also marked with pearly tints? I gave the bag a shake, trying to get a better look. Which got me nowhere when it came to size differences, and as for pearly tints, I saw none. But surely if I examined them more closely, especially around the hinge part, I'd spot a few chips made by my shucking knife and—

I heard footsteps coming from the dining room, quickly shut the fridge and zipped back to the dishwasher—almost tripping over Pendleton, dozing in a patch of sunlight—and started loading. The kitchen door opened. I glanced over my shoulder. My mom. She paused, head tilted a bit, like she was studying me.

"You like it here, don't you?" she said.

"Sure," I said. "They're so nice, Aunt Jenna and Uncle Joe."

"I meant this kind of town," my mom said. "Out of the city."

"Oh, no," I said. "I love Brooklyn."

She came over, gave me a pat on the back. "Me too," she said. "I just hope . . ."

"Hope what, Mom?"

"Nothing. And that gravy boat is Wedgwood."

"Yeah?"

"Meaning it doesn't go in the dishwasher."

"Oh."

She picked up the coffeepot and headed back toward the dining room.

"I think Pendleton needs to go outside," I said, placing the gravy boat on a sideboard. "I'll do it."

"You really are helpful today," Mom said. She gave me a very nice look, and I realized she must have been thinking I was coming through for the family when we were under pressure. So I actually ended up feeling a bit bad. "But," she went on, "what makes you think he wants to go out?"

Good point. Pendleton lay with his chin flat on the floor, eyes shut, legs splayed out in total comfort.

"I can just tell."

My mom shrugged, went into the dining room. I was in motion immediately, grabbing the bag of oysters from the fridge, kneeling beside Pendleton and whispering, "Pendleton, wake up, wake up, darn it," and I knew he was awake in there, but he lay still, refusing to open his eyes or demonstrate awakeness in any way. I needed him to get up, to be my cover for going outside and finding some place to hide the bag of oysters in our rented SUV, and I needed him now.

"Pendleton!" I grabbed his collar and got him to his feet, not easy. "Please, for once, do what I say. I'll give you a treat."

No reaction, and he knew the word *treat,* beyond any

doubt. Was it possible he also knew there were no treats in this house? No time to figure that out. I pulled on the collar. Pendleton sat back, resisting with all his strength, which could be surprisingly impressive. I gave an angry jerk on the collar, lost my grip and fell on the floor, banging into the sideboard and dropping the bag of oysters. They all came tumbling out, one of them cracking open.

Yes: my oyster. The oyster inside, that I'd already cut free, came slopping out, the tiny silver heart caught in a glistening little fold. I reached over to pick it up. But Pendleton was faster. Before I knew what was happening, he'd lowered his head and—could it be true?—scarfed up the oyster and the charm. Now he was licking the spilled oyster juices off the tiles.

"Pendleton!" I scrambled over to him, took him by the mouth, tried to open his jaws. And got nowhere. Pendleton didn't try to back away or shake me off: he just sat there, jaws tightly shut, and there was nothing I could do.

I heard voices in the dining room, and chair legs scraping on the floor. I jumped up, got the remaining oysters back in the bag, stuffed them in the fridge, and was just picking up the two shell halves of the special oyster, when everyone came in from the dining room. I jammed the shell halves in my pocket.

Were they all eyeing me in a funny way?

"He didn't want to go out," I said.

"Looks like it was quite a struggle," Uncle Joe said, which was when I realized we'd broken something, something made of china, white and blue, pieces scattered all over the place, lots of them minute, the whole thing way beyond repair. No, not the Wedgwood gravy boat? But yes.

Back home, I didn't let Pendleton out of my sight. He lay on his fluffy mat in the kitchen, couldn't have looked more comfortable, eyes open and completely vacant, showing no sign of wanting or needing to go outside. After a while, his eyes slowly closed, and around that time, I heard my phone ringing in my room. I hurried upstairs and checked the screen: Silas.

"They just found an earth-sized planet no more than three hundred light years from us," he said. "Practically in the neighborhood."

"That's what you called to tell me?" I said.

"No. But I thought you'd be interested."

"Why?"

"Who wouldn't be interested?" Silas said. "Do you see what this means? The galaxy is swarming with life."

"Thanks for letting me know. I'm kind of busy right now, Silas, and—"

"One other thing," Silas said.

"What's that?"

"Remember that secondhand record store?"

"Rewind?" How could I forget Rewind, run by this old hippie who hadn't liked getting pushed around by Sheldon Gunn's New Brooklyn Redevelopment Project?

"What was the name of the arsonist dude?" Silas said. "Long nose, kind of looks like a weasel or maybe a giant rat?"

"Harry Henkel." Tut-Tut and I had caught him spreading gasoline in the basement at Rewind, tied him up, and left him for the police. "He's in jail and refusing to talk," I said. "But how do you know what he looks like? You never saw him."

"I saw his picture online," Silas said. "He's in the news—the real reason I called, actually, although big-picture-wise, it's insignificant compared to the new planet."

"Silas? What are you telling me?"

"He's out on bail."

"What? That can't be."

"I could send you the link."

"Do you realize what this means?" I said. "He's the only one of all Gunn's people who saw us. I'm talking about our faces—mine and Tut-Tut's."

"It's a big city," Silas said, "although no longer the biggest city in the world or even close. What are the chances of him running into either of you?"

"Better than if he stayed in jail," I said.

"I could work up some numbers on exactly how much better, if you like," said Silas.

I went downstairs, my mind racing. Bail: it had never even occurred to me. Now Henkel was on the loose, plus Dina DeNunzio was out there, too, digging away. And there was way more than that going wrong—my mom's job, Tut-Tut locked up, Ashanti's father. What else? Pendleton, of course.

"Hey," I said, coming into the kitchen and noticing that Pendleton's fluffy mat was unoccupied. "Where's Pendleton?"

My dad sat at the kitchen table, writing in his notebook. Did he even hear me?

"Dad! Where's Pendleton?"

He looked up, annoyed. "What was that?" he said.

"Where's Pendleton?"

"Pendleton?" He glanced around. "I think Jane took him for a walk." He turned to his notebook.

I went into the hall and checked the hook where we hung the pooper-scooper. No pooper-scooper. I grabbed my jacket and ran outside, scanning the street both ways. No sign of Mom and Pendleton.

8

The wind was picking up, icy and cold, coming from the direction of the river. Pendleton was afraid of the wind, meaning the walk would not be long. He would quickly do what he had to do in order to get back inside the house. Mom would scoop it up, drop it in a plastic bag, and then deposit the bag in the first trash bin she came to. Would I end up searching all the trash bins in the neighborhood? I glanced around, saw nothing but trash bins, like I was in some kind of nightmare. I had to beat Pendleton to the punch, if that was how to put it.

Which way to go? Uphill led to Monsieur Señor's, Local, and other places with windows that were fun to gaze into, something my mom liked to do. Downhill meant residential brownstones all the way to Vincero, a fancy restaurant we'd been to once, but never again, on account of my dad not liking the table we were given. Pendleton preferred downhill, which meant uphill going home, but he never seemed to factor that in. I ran downhill, darting once into the street to get by two young moms pushing their gigantic strollers side by side.

I came to the first corner, glanced down the side street, and yes! Mom and Pendleton, halfway along the block and coming my way. Best news of all: my mom still had the plastic bag sticking out of her coat pocket. I was on time, Pendleton dillydallying, and he was capable of dillydallying when you'd least expect it. Mom turned to him and said something, most likely, "Hurry up, for God's sake—I'm freezing," my mom being one of those people who really felt the cold.

I caught up to them. "Hey, Mom!"

She turned to me. "Robbie? Is something wrong?"

Well, yes, but of course she didn't know that. I felt bad for my mom: she was—what was the word?—vulnerable. She was vulnerable from getting fired and maybe expected any news to be not good.

"Oh, no, Mom, everything's fine. I just thought I'd maybe relieve you, on account of the cold, and all." She gazed at me like things weren't adding up, so I threw in another reason. "Besides, I was feeling kind of energetic." And why not one more? "And I was thinking of swinging by Ashanti's."

"Inside? With Pendleton?"

"Maybe better if Ashanti comes down to the street."

"I think so." My mom handed me the leash, the pooper-scooper, the plastic bag. Her cheeks were red from the cold, the look in her eyes deep and preoccupied. "Thanks, Robbie."

"No problem," I said.

She walked off, headed for our street, bent forward against the wind.

"We're going the other way," I told Pendleton, and after not too long, I had convinced him it was a good idea, or at least an idea he could live with. Two blocks down on this side street was a narrow alley, one of Pendleton's preferred spots, as I knew from experience, and totally suitable for what I had to do.

We walked toward the alley, Pendleton being Pendleton, meaning more dillydallying, plus an episode of—I wouldn't want to say cowardice, so how about untoughness?—yes, an untough episode where a dog walker approached with three tiny dogs on tiny leashes, the dogs no more than mouse-size furballs. As soon as he spotted them, Pendleton tugged me toward the nearest building, and sheltered behind the stoop. The furballs yapped at him; the dog walker herself, earbuds in her ears and dark shades over her eyes, didn't appear to notice anything.

"Sometimes, Pendleton," I began, and then stopped. I felt—actually felt through the leash—some change taking place in Pendleton. He barked, a single bark, much lower than his normal bark, and stood very straight, head up, tail up, highly alert, and even . . . intelligent.

"Pendleton?" I said. "What's with you?"

He farted. Nothing new there. Pendleton's farts were notorious in the small circle of people who'd gotten to know him. Although there was something a bit different about this one: did I detect a faint odor of oyster? I couldn't be sure. The cold wind swept the whole invisible but nasty cloud away.

I looked into his eyes. He looked into mine. Pendleton's eyes were dusty brown, the expression in them usually peaceful and kind of vague. But not now. Now his eyes were the eyes of someone on the ball and very capable. It was almost as though another being was inside his plump and furry body, a body suddenly not so plump, which was impossible.

"Pendleton?"

He raised his snout and sniffed the air, his nostrils expanding and contracting real fast. Then he growled—growls weren't at all a Pendleton thing—and began pulling me down the street.

"Whoa. Pendleton. Easy."

He didn't seem to hear me or to feel my resistance on the leash, and I was resisting pretty much to the max. We blew right past the narrow alley where I'd planned on getting the whole doing-his-business thing done, took a right at the next street and came to Hotel P.O.V.

We didn't have a whole lot of hotels in Brooklyn—not like in Manhattan—but there'd been a few built in the last year or so, and P.O.V. was the newest, and also the coolest and most expensive, according to Ashanti's mom, who'd been invited there to a fashion magazine party, which she'd left early on account of one of her headaches, but that wasn't the point. The point was that here we were in front of P.O.V., me and Pendleton, and he was headed to the front door, with me dragging along behind him.

The doorman, dressed in black, was on the street, helping someone into a taxi. Pendleton reached the door, a beautiful glass door with etched-in grapes and flowers.

"Pendleton!" I said in a sort of whispered shout that of course had no effect. He stood in front of the door, sniffing the air. After a moment or two, an old woman in a fur coat appeared in the lobby, walking a fancy dog of some tall, lean breed I didn't know. They came through the door.

"My goodness," she said, "what a ferocious-looking dog!"

Huh? "Oh, no," I told her, "he's actually a softie, like, completely," but by that time, he'd drawn me inside. I ruled out the idea that Pendleton had detected a whiff of fancy-dog scent in the air and set off to track it down: otherwise he'd have reacted to that high-bred dog. So what Pendleton was up to remained a mystery.

Meanwhile I was in the lobby of Hotel P.O.V., tucking the scooper under my jacket, out of sight. I've hardly ever stayed in a hotel, but I've been in lots of hotel lobbies, some of the fanciest in Manhattan. Back when I was a kid—meaning a younger kid than I am now—my mom and I would often cross the river on a Saturday or Sunday and go for an explore. I loved those explores, except that sometimes you had to pee, and if there are any public bathrooms in Manhattan, I never saw one. But my mom told me that all you had to do was waltz into any hotel, pass the main desk and the concierge, and soon you'd spot a brass restroom sign on the wall. There was only one trick and that was to look like you belonged.

I crossed the lobby of P.O.V., looking like I belonged. Pendleton—this new, upright, alert Pendleton, as though someone else was at the controls inside—looked like he, too, belonged. Past the concierge desk, Pendleton cut left and we entered the bar.

I hung back: no way I could look like I belonged in a bar, not without a parent. The bar at P.O.V. was a very hip, cool bar, with lots of black marble, mirrors, shiny glasses and bottles, and deep silvery shadows created by some sort of hidden light source. Pendleton sniffed the air, started pulling me toward an isolated table at the back, a table standing in one of the deepest silvery shadows. I skidded along, sort of like a water-skier. Two men dressed in dark suits sat at that table, facing each other, and both in profile to me. They were drinking colorless drinks from thick crystal glasses. One of the men, about my dad's age, had very light blond hair and a broad face that might have been handsome if it had revealed the least bit of gentleness. The other man was older, with swept-back silvery hair and a face that was handsome, kind of like the face of one of those top-hatted actors in old black-and-white movies. And this face did seem to have some gentleness in it, although I knew that was a lie. The older man was Sheldon Gunn.

Sheldon Gunn: just about the last person on earth I wanted to see. He knew nothing about my role in what had gone down on his yacht, *Boffo,* hadn't seen me on board, although I'd caught a glimpse of him: all that is too complicated to explain now. But we'd actually met once before that, when I'd been walking with my mom and we'd run into one of the Jaggers and Tulkinghorn partners, out on some sort of strategy trip with Sheldon Gunn. What were the chances he'd remember me? Maybe not great, except that Pendleton had been with me that time, too.

As for Pendleton, this strange new Pendleton, he had no fear about meeting Sheldon Gunn again, actually seemed very eager for it. And not in a good way. He started growling—a low, hostile growl that threatened to grow much louder—and relentlessly pulled me directly toward Sheldon Gunn, sitting maybe twenty feet away, tops. With that extra strength desperation gives you—and just as Sheldon Gunn's head started turning in our direction—I yanked Pendleton into a little alcove cut in the wall.

I stood motionless and silent, holding Pendleton on the shortest possible leash. He showed no inclination toward silence himself, keeping up that low growling, deep in his throat. But over the growling, maybe because of some weird acoustical thing going on in the bar, I could hear Sheldon Gunn quite clearly. His voice was hard to forget: smooth and educated, like a lot of voices heard in some parts of the city, but with an added overtone that made it clear he was better than you.

"You can't imagine how these things work in America," he said.

"Explain, please," said the other man. Only two words, but enough for me to know he spoke with a Russian accent, as anyone who'd explored around Brooklyn a bit could have told you.

"This researcher, for example," Gunn said. "If he can establish certain things, he could make a lot of trouble for us."

"But those are ancient things!" said the Russian man.

"Makes them all the more potent, if anything," Gunn said.

The Russian man snorted. "In Moscow this would all be over very quick."

"I'm aware of that," Gunn said. "Why do you imagine you're on the payroll?"

"Sorry, boss."

"I'll be in touch," Gunn said. A chair scraped. Meaning Gunn was on the move, about to go right by the alcove? What if he looked my way? I glanced wildly around, saw that the alcove led to the bathrooms, women's to the right. I darted through the door—Pendleton coming willingly, for some reason—and locked it behind us. Pendleton, quickly solving the mystery of this mood change for me, went over to the toilet and started slurping from the bowl, suddenly thirsty. I'd caught a break.

When he'd finished drinking, he headed right for the door.

"No way." I told him, trying for fierceness and quiet in the same breath. I held him back with all my strength. "Sit." He refused to sit. "Treat. A whole box of treats." But he knew I had no treats on me. He tugged at the leash, tugged and growled, then without warning stopped all that and went back to sniffing the air. After that, he made an unhappy, high-pitched little noise and sat.

"Pendleton? He's gone? Is that it? What's with your sense of smell all of a sudden? Sense of smell never being one of your strong points."

Pendleton began to scratch himself behind the ear.

Much more like him. I gave him a little tug, then stepped back into the alcove and peeked around the corner.

The broad-faced blond man was still at his table, bent over his phone, but there was no sign of Sheldon Gunn. Coast clear. I turned the other way, all set to zip on out of that bar, out of P.O.V., and onto the safety of the street, when I saw, coming my way, the actual very last person on earth I wanted to see: rat-faced Harry Henkel, the arsonist, freshly out on bail.

I ducked back into the alcove, heart pounding. Harry Henkel didn't know my name or who I was, but he sure knew my face, and also, unlike Sheldon Gunn, knew we were enemies. Was *enemy* too strong a word? I couldn't think of a better one.

He went right past us, almost within touching distance, walking fast and raising his hand, as though greeting somebody. I heard him say, "Mr. Kolnikov?"

"Henkel?" said the Russian man.

Over at the bar, a woman rose and started walking my way, headed for the bathroom. I glanced around the corner again. Mr. Kolnikov, the Russian, was still in his seat. Henkel had joined him, sitting with his back to us. Break number two, and how could I count on another? We split, me and Pendleton, not looking back.

9

We walked fast, side by side, Pendleton back to radiating so many un-Pendleton things: strength, purpose, intelligence, swagger. The charm had worked on Pendleton once before, making him uncharacteristically fierce, but not doing this complete upgrade. But then the charm hadn't been inside him, and now it was.

As for me, I felt scared and confused. Sheldon Gunn had had some sort of meeting with this Mr. Kolnikov guy and then Mr. Kolnikov had met with Harry Henkel. Why? What was going on? And did the fact that those little sit-downs had taken place within a fifteen-minute walk from where I lived mean anything?

"What's going on, Pendleton?" I said, first time I'd ever actually consulted him on anything, a completely whacked-out thing to do. He regarded me without turning his head much, the way dogs can do, and again I caught this strange expression—like he was possessed, and not only that, but possessed by someone or something that actually could have answered my question, if only Pendleton were capable of speech.

We came to the narrow alley. Normally I'd have told him, "Pendleton, go on in there, get it done," but now all I said was, "Pendleton?" What did he want to do? What was on his mind?

He turned into the alley. I bent and unclipped the leash. Pendleton preferred a bit of space for this sort of thing, and I didn't blame him.

He moved toward a grate in the pavement, sniffed at it.

"Not there," I said. "Please."

He kept going, almost as though he understood, even followed my reasoning, had no wish to see me descending into the sewers of Brooklyn.

"Robbie," I said, to myself but aloud, "get a grip." Pendleton, not stopping, gave me a backward glance as though out of concern for me talking to myself; totally impossible. He came to a small Dumpster and disappeared behind it. I started moving in that direction, not quickly, giving him time. I got there just as he was reappearing, out from behind the Dumpster.

"Success?" I said. "All done?"

Pendleton yawned, a very big, wide-mouth yawn, and then looked around. Kind of blankly? I thought so. He gave himself a good shake and looked around again. Yes, definitely blank. Plus he was standing in an unathletic sort of way, one paw turned out, no longer giving off strong, capable vibes, even seeming not quite all there. Pendleton was back to normal.

I walked around to the other side of the Dumpster, and there found indisputable evidence of Pendleton's performance. What I didn't see—and what I'd been hoping to see out in the open, without any further effort required from me—was the tiny silver heart. What if it wasn't there? Or still inside Pendleton? Or he'd concealed it in his mouth and spat it out somewhere, which was his MO with every pill the vet ever prescribed for him?

I checked around, spotted one those sticks for stirring paint. Perfect. I picked it up, knelt down, got to work, carefully poking around. And yes! There it was! I scooped the silver heart into the scooper, mixed in some crusty snow from the snowbank against the nearest building wall, got it nice and clean. Then I took off my glove and picked up my charm—very carefully, ready in case it started in on one of its tricks, like heating up, or giving me a jolt, or making me see perfectly without my glasses. But the charm did none of those things, just lay inert on my palm, a normal silver charm you'd hang on a bracelet. One thing I remembered about it was how it had felt surprisingly heavy. Ashanti had thought it might be platinum, but Silas said more likely palladium or rhodium, which I'd never even heard of, and had wanted to run some tests. But now it didn't feel surprisingly heavy at all; if anything, it felt lighter than it should.

What was going on? Had the charm lost its magic? Or was the magic still around, but now absorbed somehow by Pendleton? I glanced at him, at the moment doing two things at once, namely licking his muzzle and gazing at the sky—not looking the least bit magical—and then pocketed the silver heart.

We sat around the desk in the abandoned warehouse on Sherwood Street, our HQ—me, Ashanti, Silas. On the desk lay the silver heart. For about the zillionth time, Silas gave it a little poke.

"Nada," he said. "Zip, zilch, zero, reaction-wise."

"Tell us something we don't know," Ashanti said.

"Sure," said Silas. "You can't determine both the exact position and the exact speed of a particle at the same instant."

"What the hell are you talking about?" Ashanti said.

"Admit you didn't know that," Silas said.

"Don't know what?" When Ashanti starts getting mad, her chin tilts up and her eyes narrow in a way that would make anyone with half a brain back off.

But Silas, with his brain and a half, always seemed to miss the signal. "What I just said. Heisenberg's Uncertainty Principle. You didn't know it. Ergo I told you something you didn't know."

"Silas?" I said. "Please don't ever say ergo again."

"Why not? It's a perfectly good—"

Ashanti raised her hand, raised it pretty much in the form of a fist.

"But there are plenty of synonyms," Silas said, "so no biggie."

We all gazed at the charm.

"Go over the whole oyster thing again," Ashanti said.

I went over the oyster thing again. When I finished, Silas said, "Anybody got any gum?"

"How come you never do?" Ashanti said, handing him a stick.

"I had some," Silas said. "My brother took it."

"Thaddeus is around?" Ashanti said. Thaddeus was Silas's genius older brother; I'd never met him.

"Got out of rehab," Silas said.

"How's he doing?" I said.

"Doesn't say much," Silas said. "Eats a lot of peanut butter, the chunky kind. Right out of the jar. My mom hates that, but she doesn't say anything."

Even though Silas was such a pain, I felt bad for him at that moment. He never saw his father—his parents had been divorced for a long time, and he never talked about his dad.

Here was something I was learning about Ashanti and me: our minds often seemed to be heading in the same direction. The big difference showed up when our minds got there. For example, Ashanti now leaned forward and said, "What's the deal with your father?" Which was something I'd never have dared to ask.

Silas, right in the middle of cracking his gum, went still. "My father?"

"Yeah."

"My parents are divorced—you know that."

Ashanti nodded. "How come?"

"How come my parents got divorced?" Silas said. He flushed from his neck up to the top of his forehead, all his freckles turning white at the same time. "What's it to you?" I had some notion about that, but of course there was no way Silas could have known about the text message Ashanti had seen and what was really on her mind.

Ashanti shrugged. "Nothing. Don't be so touchy."

"Touchy?" He turned to me. "Robbie? Was I being touchy?"

"Let's just cool it," I said. "We've got bigger problems." I gestured at the charm. And then there was Tut-Tut, problem two. Tied for first, actually. Or maybe number one all by himself.

Ashanti and Silas glared at each other for another second or two, then both turned to the charm.

"How do we know it's the same one?" Silas said.

"What do you mean?" I said.

"Where's the power?" Silas said. He poked the silver heart. "That head-zapping thing? Gonzo." The head zap happened when the power entered you, an instant ice cream headache that faded fast. After that, the power expressed itself in different ways—mental telepathy when it came to Silas.

"Think something, Silas," I said.

"Okay," he said, "I'm thinking about the dark side of the moon."

"Not out loud," I said. "And touch the charm while you're thinking."

"And don't think anything dorky," Ashanti said.

"What's dorky about the dark side of the moon?" Silas shifted the space heater a little more his way.

"Close your eyes," I said. "Think. Not about the moon."

Silas closed his eyes. "Not about the moon at all, or just not the dark side?"

"I'm going to smack you," Ashanti said.

Silas shrank back, closing his eyes even tighter. "No moon of any kind. No planets, no asteroids, no comets, no quasars, no—"

"Silas!"

"Okay, okay! All right. Here we go. Thought, coming up."

He went still, and certainly appeared to be thinking, but no thought jumped the gap from him to me. My mind, wide open, remained blank.

"Ashanti?" I said. "Anything?"

"Nope."

Silas opened his eyes. "You didn't get that?" he said.

We shook our heads.

"What was it?" I asked Silas.

"Do I have to tell?"

"What is it about you, Silas?" Ashanti said.

"Like in what way?"

"The way that makes me want to dangle you out the window by your ankles?"

Which was impossible, the single window here at HQ being boarded over, but Silas glanced nervously in that direction anyway.

"Let's try again," I said, "this time with all of us touching the charm."

Not easy, what with the size of the charm, but we all managed to get a fingertip on it. Silas's skin felt cold, Ashanti's hot.

"On three," Silas said. We all closed our eyes. "Anda one, anda two, anda three!"

At first my mind was blank again. Then, all of a sudden, I thought about my mom losing her job, but not in Silas's voice—I hadn't even told him about it yet. Meanwhile, Ashanti was sounding angry. "Silas—were you thinking about my mom?"

"Huh?" said Silas. "How could I be thinking about your mom? I don't know her from Adam."

We all opened our eyes.

"You thought about your mom?" I said to Ashanti.

She nodded.

"So did I," I said. "I mean, I thought about my mom, not yours." We both turned to Silas.

"I wasn't thinking about anybody's mom or moms in general."

"What were you thinking of?" I said.

"Do I have to tell?" he said again. Silas could be very circular.

"Silas?"

"I was thinking about yo-yos," he said quickly, "if you must know."

"Yo-yos?"

"Giant yo-yos, actually," he said. "Activated by tidal forces, they might be an efficient energy multiplier."

We gazed at him. Yo-yos were circular; it was sort of uncanny.

"Just a thought," he said. "But it didn't get through, huh?"

We withdrew our hands from the silver heart. It lay on the desk, looking totally everyday.

"Let's admit it," Silas said. "This is not our charm."

"But I told you," I said, counting off the points on my fingers. "It sort of . . . got Pendleton to lead me to that hotel."

"We don't know that," Silas said. "Dogs have a great sense of smell. And what about all the for-sure things the charm used to do? Like the soaring, the laser thing, all that?"

"I don't know," I said. "Maybe it's been changed."

"Changed?" said Ashanti.

"Even weakened," I went on. "From a sort of ordeal—falling to the bottom of the ocean, getting swallowed by an oyster."

"Or," Silas said.

"Or what?" I said.

"Or maybe, you know," Silas said, "you kind of imagined it."

"Imagined what? I'm telling you, I—" At that moment, I felt Ashanti's eyes on me. I turned toward her. "You think that too? I imagined it?"

Ashanti met my gaze, didn't say anything.

"Oh, my God," I said. "You don't even believe I found it in the oyster? You think I went out and bought it somewhere?"

"I didn't say that," Ashanti said.

"But it is an interesting idea," said Silas.

I rose. "So I'm lying?" I said. "What kind of friends are you?"

Silas started flushing again. Ashanti took my arm.

"Aw, come on," she said. "I know you wouldn't lie. Not on purpose."

"What does that mean?"

"Nothing. Forget I said it. You're not lying. Period."

"Thanks a bunch."

"Hey, Robbie, I'm sorry," Ashanti said.

I took a deep breath, tried to calm down. "You don't need to say you're sorry."

"Too late. Just sit back down. We have to think."

We thought. All at once, Ashanti snapped her fingers. Unlike Silas, she was one of those real talented finger snappers—it sounded like a gunshot. "I've got it," she said. "We'll invent a test for the charm. To see if it's really real."

Silas rubbed his hands together. "Now we're cooking," he said.

"What kind of test?"

"Standardized," Silas said. "Big time."

"Shut up," Ashanti said. She poked the charm. "We know that the charm—the real charm—reacts to injustice, right?"

"So we have to find an injustice to expose it to?" Silas said.

We all thought of Tut-Tut at the exact same moment.

10

"And another thing," Silas said, as we walked toward the subway entrance, the wind funneling down the street, right in our faces, "where's the leather bracelet the charm used to hang from?"

"I don't know," I said. "Probably on the bottom of the ocean. What difference does it make?"

"Maybe a shark ate it," Silas said.

"So?" I said.

"Nothing," said Silas. "Just brainstorming."

"Brainstorming is a group activity," Ashanti said. "You can't brainstorm on your own."

"I do it all the time," Silas said.

"Snot's hanging out of your nose," Ashanti said.

We entered the station, swiped our cards—Silas didn't have one, so I swiped for him, too—and jumped on a train. Silas wiped his nose on the back of one of his mittens.

"You got new mittens?" I said. His mittens were brown, the same color as those he'd given Tut-Tut, but a price tag hung from one of them.

"Yeah," he said. "Like 'em?"

"What's wrong with gloves?" Ashanti said.

"Where do you want me to start?" said Silas.

"Nowhere."

At that moment, a red-eyed toothless man entered from the next car, shuffling to some rhythm in his head and shaking a paper cup. Nobody in the car put any money in it; they all just stared straight ahead like they couldn't see him, one of those city techniques we all learn young. My parents said giving money to street people was really not a good way to help them, but I sometimes did anyway—just a quarter or two—which maybe had something to do with why I'd gotten the charm in the first place.

I know you. You're the girlie who dropped eighty-five cents in the cup. And sixty another time.

But not to this guy: he was too scary. He came to the end of the car, shuffled into the next one.

Ashanti glanced around, spoke low so no one but us could hear. "Did it do anything when he went by?" Ashanti said.

"The charm?" I said. "I didn't feel anything." I put my hand in my pocket, felt it: body temperature.

"Maybe you should wear it on this," Ashanti said, taking off her little gold neck chain.

"Oh, no," I said. "I couldn't do that."

"Because silver doesn't match with gold?" Silas said. We both looked at him. "Just trying to understand girls," he explained. "Your thought processes, that kind of thing."

I started laughing. Not in a mocking way or anything like that. It was just plain funny. Ashanti joined in. We laughed and laughed.

"What's funny?" Silas said. "It can't be done—right?—understanding girls? Is that the joke? Am I close?" Now he laughed too, and also started looking pretty pleased with himself. Ashanti took the charm, hooked it onto the necklace, clasped it around my neck. It felt good.

We rolled into a station, squealed to a stop, maybe squealing even louder than usual. The doors opened. There were people on the platform but none of them got on. The doors stayed open. An announcement came over the speakers. For some reason, my parents could never make out a single word of these subway announcements. This one was all about some problem down the track and our train no longer being in service. We went up to the street and headed for a station with access to other lines.

It happened to be the nearest station to Thatcher, less than two blocks from the school, meaning we had to go right past the corner where the homeless woman had dropped the charm, which might have seemed strange since I'd just been thinking about her, but for some reason did not, even seemed right. What would happen if I walked right over the exact spot in the gutter where it had fallen? Would the charm just hang there around my neck or would it . . . do something?

No way to find out. Police barricades were up all around the corner, and some kind of demonstration was going on. Not a big one: maybe a dozen people, a few carrying homemade signs reading SLOW DOWN—GREED KILLS and SAVE OUR NEIGHBORHOOD. On the other side of the barricade, the nearby buildings were all blocked off by scaffolding that must have gone up over the weekend. A bunch of cops—way more cops than demonstrators—stood in front of the barricades. Behind the barricades, I caught glimpses of a cameraman shooting an interview. The interviewer, wearing a red leather jacket and a long black scarf, was Dina DeNunzio. She seemed to be interviewing two people. One, bareheaded, his longish silver hair ruffling in the wind, was Sheldon Gunn. The other, a tall, golden-haired woman with a strong-featured face, looked familiar.

We went closer, crossing the street and standing just behind the demonstrators. I didn't know about

Ashanti and Silas, but for me it was like being pulled by a magnet.

"Who's that blond woman?" I said.

"She's not really blond," Ashanti said. "I saw this whole thing on Celebuzz."

"What's that?" said Silas.

"This stupid site," I said. "But who is she?"

"The mayor," Ashanti said.

"The mayor of New York?"

"The one and only," said Ashanti. "Bought with her own money, as Mr. Stinecki says."

Silas stood on his tiptoes, tried to see better, lost his balance. "What's going on?" he said.

One of the demonstrators turned to us. He wore his hair in two long braids, some white hairs woven in with others that were sort of a faded reddish.

"Desecration," he said.

Which was a word I didn't know, leaving me in the dark.

Maybe this guy realized that, because he went on, "He wants to block the sun."

"Who?" I said.

"Block the sun?" said Silas, frowning the way he did when some objection was forming in his mind.

The braided guy, who hadn't noticed Silas till that point—his focus being more on me and Ashanti—turned to him. "That's the psychological underpinning—to replace the gods and become them yourself." He was a real fast talker, like he could hardly keep up with what was unfolding in his mind. "In more pedestrian terms, Sheldon Gunn, fresh off the New Brooklyn fiasco, traded a boatload of air rights he controlled in Manhattan for permission to build the tallest tower in America, right here in Brook—" He blinked once or twice, looking confused. "Silas?" he said.

"Huh?" said Silas.

The braided guy's eyes softened. He bent down a bit, hands on his knees, eye level with Silas. "You've grown," he said.

Their two faces were close together. Silas had a round face, while the man's face was kind of long, plus there were other differences, like Silas basically had a cheerful face and this man did not, but there was one amazing similarity. Maybe it's not nice to separate people's physical features into good and bad, and therefore I'm not always nice, because it's a habit I fall into sometimes, and in Silas's case, his best feature was his eyes. They were a very light brown, almost honey-colored, and quite prominent without being the stick-out-too-much kind. The eyes of the braided guy were just about identical.

"D-d-," Silas began, and for a crazy second I had the whacked-out thought that the charm was not only back in action but had turned against us, its first nasty trick being to spread Tut-Tut's stuttering to Silas. But the truth was almost stranger than that. "D-Dad?" Silas said.

"What?" said Ashanti. I gave her a quick elbow jab of the silencing type.

"It's, uh, been some time," said the guy, speaking more slowly now, and way less confidently. "Perhaps—no, quite certainly—too long a time."

Silas drew back. His round face wasn't so round all of a sudden. He almost looked like another kid, a much harder one. "Too long a time for what?" he said.

"For a get-together."

"Get-together?"

"A visit, maybe an outing of sorts." The braided guy bit his lip, chapped and cracked from the cold. "How's—how's your mother?"

"Ask her," Silas said, staring right into the braided guy's eyes. The braided guy—no doubt in my mind now that he was Silas's dad—looked away. Silas—this super-Silas or maybe anti-Silas—gestured at our surroundings. "And isn't this an outing?"

Silas's dad winced like he'd felt a sudden pain. "Well, yes, but not exactly what I meant." Some kind of uproar started up over by the barricades, with lots of shouting and nasty words. Silas's dad glanced quickly around. "What are you doing here, anyway?"

Silas shrugged. "Just hangin' out with my friends."

Another super-Silas remark, almost cool. What was with him?

"Are you going to introduce me?" his dad said.

"Sure," said Silas. "These are a couple of my friends."

"Hi," his dad said to me and Ashanti. "I'm Jim Wilders, Silas's somewhat wayward father."

"Robbie," I said. "Um, nice to meet you."

"Ashanti," said Ashanti, adding, "What are air rights?" in that direct way of hers.

"Good question," Mr. Wilders said. "The people who used to live right here where we're standing—my people—never even thought of owning a piece of the earth, let alone its air. Now owning air is just one more way to leverage money out of nothing. Sheldon Gunn makes the money, the mayor gets his support, and the rich swarm into this neighborhood, forcing out the poor. That's the system."

"Your people?" I said. "Did you used to live here or . . ."

Silas was shaking his head in a disgusted sort of way.

"I'm talking spiritually," Mr. Wilders said, "which seems to annoy Silas, just the way it annoyed his—"

A gust of wind blew across the street, parting my jacket and lifting the charm up around to the side of my neck. Mr. Wilders's eyes locked on it right away. I straightened out the chain and pulled the charm back down, closing my jacket. Mr. Wilders seemed about to ask me something, but at that moment a bunch of cops came toward us from the barricades.

"Off the street! Everybody off the street!"

The demonstrators didn't move. Mr. Wilders wheeled around, his braids flying, planted himself right in front of the biggest cop and bellowed, "This is our street. We have every right."

"Telling you one more time."

Wilders turned up the volume even more. "We have every right."

In a flash, the cops were on him. There was a big struggle, furious words getting shouted back and forth, and then they clamped the cuffs on him. As they dragged him away to an NYPD van, he looked at Silas, his eyes full of complicated emotions I didn't understand. Silas looked away.

The crowd, with us in it, got pushed back onto the sidewalk, clearing the way for Sheldon Gunn, the mayor, and other well-dressed people to drive off in limos. That was when I finally noticed the most obvious thing about the whole scene, what anyone else would have noticed from the get-go, namely the yellow crane that rose high above the scaffolding, bearing a huge red banner with gold lettering: GUNN TOWER. It snapped so loudly in the wind I could hear it from way down on the ground.

I lowered my eyes, found Dina DeNunzio among the people still by the barricades, watched her getting into the TV truck. A mistake: some people knew when they were being watched. Dina was one of them. She paused, scanned our side of the street, looked me right in the eye. Then she raised up her index finger to the driver, like she was telling him to wait.

"Let's go," I said.

Ashanti was on the move at once, but Silas, gazing at his feet, hadn't heard. I took him by the hand. We went.

"Silas?" I said when we'd gone a few blocks. "What's the story?"

"Huh?"

Ashanti, still a step or two in front of us, stopped, turned, and put a hand on Silas's chest. "Someone as smart as you can't play dumb. It just won't fly."

"*You* think I'm smart?" Silas said.

"Shut up," she told him. "Shut up and spill the beans."

"About what?"

"The dude with the braids, of course," Ashanti said. "Is he really your father?"

Silas gave a little nod.

"And?"

"And they got divorced, like I already maybe mentioned."

"Know something?" Ashanti said. "You're the most pigheaded person I ever met."

"Then allow me to introduce you to yourself," said Silas.

"Whoa," I said. "Just stop, both of you." I tugged them into the recessed doorway of an out-of-business clothing store. We were sheltered from the wind in a quiet little space, close together, our breath clouds merging into one. "Let's have it, Silas," I said.

"In A-through-Z format, if possible," Ashanti added.

Silas thought about that. I could see he was very upset, but still his mind couldn't help running on Silas-type tracks. At that moment, I liked him a whole lot.

"Z would have to be the divorce," he said. "And we'll make A when they met, my mom and him, which was in college. How about F for when Thaddeus came along, and X for me, four years later? In between F and X was when he went to grad school—totally supported by my mother—and got obsessed with Native American history. Like, to the point of wanting to be Indian himself. He did all this research and, for a while, thought he'd found a Mohawk ancestor, but it all fell apart, and after that, he started to get mean. My mom—call this Y—told him he should see a therapist. He hit her—"

"Oh, my God!" Ashanti and I said, speaking as one.

"And she threw him out. Z."

"That's terrible," I said.

Silas shrugged. "It was tough on Thaddeus," he said.

"I was too young to get affected." But as he spoke, tears welled up and spilled down his cheeks. He didn't make a crying sound, or even look particularly sad, but those tears kept coming. Ashanti wrapped her arms around him and then tilted her head down a bit—she was much taller than Silas—and kissed him on the forehead. Silas looked shocked. His tears dried up fast.

"He does send child support," Silas said when we were back in motion, headed for the Flatbush Family Detention Center. "He's got a good job."

"Doing what?" said Ashanti.

"He works on the Native American floor in the museum and teaches a bit. Thaddeus says he has a pretty cool apartment in Greenpoint."

"Let me guess," Ashanti said. "Thaddeus wanted to move in with him, and your father turned him down."

Silas's eyebrows rose in surprise. "How do you know that?"

"Just makes sense," Ashanti said. "Fathers being what they are."

"What do you mean?" Silas said.

"Forget it," Ashanti told him.

By the time we got to the detention center, the sky was darkening—so early—and tiny pellets of something between rain and snow were swirling in the air. From somewhere not far away came the sound of a Christmas carol being played on a tinkly instrument. We walked quickly past the entrance and turned the corner, the tall, grimy wall rising on our left. We came to the archway and peered through the two sets of bars into the barren yard. No one was there.

"This is around when we came the last time," I said.

"No logic there," said Silas.

Ashanti ignored him—ignored both of us—stepped right up to the bars and yelled, "Tut-Tut! Tut-Tut!"

"What makes you think he can even—" Silas began.

And then Tut-Tut came running, a smile spreading on his face. He looked skinnier than before, wore the same too-big hoodie, torn jeans, my old laceless sneakers—and no mittens.

"Tut-Tut," I said, "where are the mittens?"

A totally dumb remark, like I was his mother or something and, worse, the nagging kind.

His smile faded. "Th-th-th-th-th-," he began, then glanced over his shoulder.

"Someone stole them?" I said.

"Y-y-y-ye-ye-ye-ye . . ."

A jet of anger went right through me. I'd never felt so purely angry in my life. So it was kind of surprising that the charm had no reaction, lay cold against my skin.

"I could give him these," Silas said, "but they'd just steal them again."

"Forget it," Ashanti said. "We're here to bust him out."

Tut-Tut's eyebrows rose in surprise. "H-h-h-h-?"

"We've got the charm," Ashanti said. "If this isn't injustice what is? All set?"

Tut-Tut nodded a series of fast little nods.

"Anybody around back there?" Ashanti said.

Tut-Tut looked around again, shook his head.

"Robbie?" said Ashanti.

I moved closer and examined the bars. If I made four unwelds, if that was what to call them, a nice-sized square would open up, plenty of room for Tut-Tut to squeeze through. I held the charm up close to the intersection of two waist-level bars. Now all we needed was heat. Magic time.

11

Nothing happened. Not one single thing. What had I been expecting? Probably some sort of energy shining out of the charm, melting right through the metal, opening a Tut-Tut-sized hole. But anything would have done—Tut-Tut rising up and soaring over the wall, the wall itself crumbling down, a sinkhole appearing in the ground under the archway. The charm reacted to injustice and if Tut-Tut being locked up in this horrible place for nothing he'd ever done wasn't injustice, then what was?

"Nothing seems to be happening," Silas said. "At least not noticeably."

"We can see that," Ashanti said. "The question is—what are we going to do about it?"

We gazed at Tut-Tut. He gazed at us. The tinkly Christmas carol music grew a bit louder. That made me think about *A Christmas Carol*—even though I couldn't remember if there were any Christmas carols in the movie—and my dad saying it was sentimental crap. Not the moment for thoughts like that, but the mind wasn't so easy to control, at least not mine. Was Sheldon Gunn like Scrooge? I tried to imagine Sheldon Gunn realizing the error of his ways like Scrooge in the end, and couldn't. My dad was right.

"Here's a logical thought," Silas said. "The charm has an injustice trigger point, and we're not there."

"You're saying this isn't unjust enough?" Ashanti said.

"Logic is saying it," Silas said. "I'm just the messenger."

Tut-Tut laughed. A quiet little laugh. So nice to hear—there was no impediment to his laughter—but laughing at a time like this? Seeing something funny in the situation? We had to get him out.

"Maybe," I said, "it's not injustice that sets the charm off, but our reaction."

"Our reaction to the injustice?" Ashanti said. "How much we feel it?"

"Something like that," I said.

"Makes sense," Ashanti said.

"In what way?" said Silas.

She reached out toward him. He flinched, but she was only taking his hand. She held mine, too.

"Close your eyes," she said. "On three. Feel it. One, two, three."

I closed my eyes and right away pictured this quick

sketch Tut-Tut had once made for me, a sketch about how he'd lost his parents on the way to America. Just a few penciled strokes in a spiral notebook: a rough, empty ocean; a broken mast adrift in the waves; a small figure clinging to it. And from deep inside me this powerful feeling came rising up, part anger, part pity, and other parts I couldn't name. At the same time, Ashanti squeezed my hand tight, and I just knew something similar was going on in her. But from the charm, still in my other hand, still aimed at the bars, I felt nothing.

I opened my eyes. Nothing it was.

"Next theory," Silas said.

"How about you coming up with it?" I said, getting rid of some of my anger on him.

"Yeah," said Ashanti, maybe doing the same thing. "I felt nothing from you. What were you thinking of?"

"Injustice, just like you," Silas said.

"What specifically?" said Ashanti.

Silas opened his mouth, hesitated.

"Spill it," I told him.

"I was thinking about Étienne Lenoir," Silas said.

"Who the hell is he?" said Ashanti.

"The inventor of the internal combustion engine, but he died poor and no one remembers."

I wanted to strangle him.

"I want to strangle you," Ashanti said.

Silas backed away. "What? What? The inventor of

the internal combustion engine dies poor? Automobiles, anybody? GM, Ford, Honda, BMW? The interstate highway system? Rest stops? Hello?"

"Zip it," I said. "This isn't getting us anywhere." I looked through the bars at Tut-Tut, the double pattern of steel crisscrossing his whole body and face. "Tut-Tut?" I said. "Any ideas?"

He shook his head. It was getting darker. I remembered this same sort of sky on our first visit to the detention center, when an angry guard had called Tut-Tut inside. That could happen again at any second. And then what? We were helpless!

The wind blew stronger, bringing that tinkly Christmas carol with it, more distinct now. I was thinking so hard—and getting nowhere—that I barely noticed Tut-Tut cocking his head to the sound. And then he opened his mouth and began to sing.

"It came upon a midnight clear, that glorious song of old."

I'd forgotten that when Tut-Tut sang, the stuttering went away, also forgotten how well he did it, hitting all the notes right in the middle, something I'd been unable to do in my one year of forced piano lessons, and the piano was supposed to hit the notes in the middle for you. But there was no time to think about any of that, because when Tut-Tut got to *midnight,* the charm vibrated very slightly in my hand, and I heard a heavy metallic click, more like a clonk, the kind of sound a real heavy lock might make. And the next moment, the two gates, inner and outer, swung open.

"Wha-wha-wha-," Tut-Tut began. An alarm went off somewhere behind him, loud and piercing *Bwa-BWAAA bwa-BWAAA bwa-BWAAA.*

"Tut-Tut! Run!"

He ran to us, through the gates. I grabbed his hand. "Come on!"

We took off, not toward the front of the detention center, but the other way, down this side street. Ashanti sprinted out in front, with me and Tut-Tut not far behind. I glanced back. Could it be true? Silas wasn't actually running, just walking fast?

"Silas! Run!"

He picked up the pace. Was it running? Ms. Kleinberg, my basketball coach at Thatcher, said that in running there's a moment in every stride when both feet are off the ground. By that definition, no, Silas was not running.

"Run!"

"I'm running, I'm running! I'm just not that speedy." *Huff puff.* "Relatively."

"Both feet off the ground! Run!"

"Both feet off the ground?" He tried it, and all of a

sudden—for the first time in his life?—Silas was running. Not fast, not average, not just below average—slow, real slow, but running. Silas: probably the smartest person I'd ever met, but he'd had to be taught how to run.

We ran. From behind came the *bwa-BWAAA* of the alarm and some shouting. I glanced back, saw two uniformed guards in the distance. Silas, all red-faced and sweaty, still far ahead of them, had somehow discovered a running style that kept both feet off the ground way too long, meaning his horizontal progress was even worse than I'd thought.

"Silas! Hurry! We've got to get around the corner."

"This hurts my ankles."

"Run! They're catching up!"

"They are?" Silas turned his head to glance back. A mistake: I knew that from the get-go, saw the whole thing coming. He tripped over his own feet and sprawled in the gutter. The two guards picked up the pace, and now more guards came into view behind them.

"Silas! Get up!"

Silas seemed to be moving in slow motion. He rolled over, sat up, and—oh, no! was it possible? Yes: he was tying his shoelace.

"Silas!" I was so busy yelling at Silas and basically going out of my mind, that I completely missed Tut-Tut coming from the other direction. He blew right by me, racing back at top speed to rescue Silas.

"Tut-Tut—no!"

He didn't seem to hear me. He reached Silas, pulled him to his feet, and started tugging him along. The guards were closing in, less than half a block away, but there was still a chance, if only we could make it to the next corner. Then, from out of nowhere, a green car with a flashing roof light zoomed up, right beside Tut-Tut and Silas, and a uniformed man jumped out while it was still moving. He grabbed Tut-Tut with both hands and threw him into the car. It squealed around in a tight U-turn and sped off the other way.

The other guards surrounded Silas. I crept closer, Ashanti right behind me. Maybe they didn't realize we'd all been together: they showed no interest in me and Ashanti. They glared down at Silas, looking real mad. Silas looked real small. He tilted his head up to face them.

"I'm a citizen," he said. "I have rights."

"You have the right to have the crap beaten out of you," one of the guards said. "What's your relationship to that little escape artist?"

"He's a kid I know."

"From where?"

"Here," said Silas. "Brooklyn. Where he lives."

"Not for long," said another guard. "He'll be back down under the palm trees so fast it'll make your head spin. Now tell us how you got him out of the yard."

"Uh," said Silas. "Me? I didn't do anything."

"No? Then how'd he get the gate to open up?"

Silas paused. From thirty or forty feet away, I could feel him thinking. "We closed our eyes and willed it to happen."

The guards seemed to swell up. "You making fun of us?"

"No, no," said Silas, shaking his head violently back and forth.

"What's your name?"

"Silas."

"Let's see some ID, Silas."

"I don't have any," he told them. "I'm a home-school kid."

The guards looked at one another. "What a crazy city," one said.

They shuffled around, starting to lose interest in Silas. "Could be a software glitch," one said.

"Or a hacker."

All of a sudden, Silas looked intrigued. "A hacker?" he said, at the exact moment when he should have been keeping his stupid mouth shut.

They focused on him again. "Huh? What are you saying?"

"I never thought of hacking the system," Silas said. "It didn't even occur to me. Can you believe it?"

The guards gazed down at him, now like he was some strange specimen. "Are all homeschooled kids as weird as you?" one said.

When the guards left, we gathered together without a word and got on the first bus that came along. We sat by ourselves at the back, feeling dismal.

"What are we going to do?" Ashanti said.

"We could go back tomorrow," I said. "Take another swing at it."

"Meaning he sings 'It Came Upon a Midnight Clear' again?" she said. "And what makes you think they'll even let him in the yard anymore?"

"Don't get mad at me," I said.

"I think I've got a high ankle sprain," Silas said. "That means ligament damage. In case anybody's interested."

No one was. We rode in silence, our minds—mine, at least, on Tut-Tut. Out on the street, normal life went on. A man and woman emerged from a Chinese restaurant. A taxi pulled up. The man—very-good looking, with beautifully shaped hands that reminded me of Ashanti's—glanced quickly around and then kissed her on the mouth. He jumped into the cab, and it sped off, the woman—also good-looking, maybe somewhat younger than the man—watching it disappear in traffic.

It hit me—for the first time! pretty late in the game!—that I'd probably have a boyfriend someday, or would want to.

"I've got an idea," I said. "How does hot chocolate sound?"

"I don't have any money," Silas said.

12

Ashanti and I got off the bus at our stop and walked home.

"He never has any money," she said.

"But his father pays child support."

"Maybe Silas is just saying that."

"Why would he?" I said.

"I don't know," she said. "When things are screwed up, they just grow more and more screwed up."

She sounded so down. I felt down myself. Coming so close to success and then failing—which was what had happened with Tut-Tut—felt way worse than just flat-out not even getting in the game. I wanted to get back in the game and fast. "I'm going to talk to my mom," I said.

"What about?"

"Tut-Tut. She's a lawyer. Maybe she'll have some ideas."

"What are you going to say?"

"He's a kid I knew at Joe Louis, and now he's in trouble."

Ashanti perked up, at least a little. "Thatcha," she said.

"Comin' atcha."

And we were high-fiving in a half-assed sort of way—by this time in front of Ashanti's stoop—when a cab pulled up and man got out, carrying a bag of Chinese takeout.

He was about my dad's age, but taller and better looking in a conventional sort of a way, with symmetrical features, kind of preppy.

"Hey, babe," he said.

"Hi, Dad," said Ashanti. "This is Robbie. Robbie, my dad."

We shook hands. His hand, beautifully shaped, was a bigger, masculine version of Ashanti's. Mine was shaking a bit.

"Nice to meet you, Robbie," he said. "I've heard a lot about you. All good."

"Uh, thanks, Mr. Marshall."

"Call me Nick."

"Um."

He shifted the takeout bag. "Join us for dinner?"

"Thanks, but . . . I should go home." I turned to Ashanti, tried to look like my normal self. "Talk to you later."

They went up the steps. I continued down the street toward my house. The news, real bad, was that I'd already seen Ashanti's dad that day, seen him from the bus. What if she'd glanced out at that moment, too? But she had not, so she'd missed the sight of her father getting into a taxi, and just before getting in, saying good-bye to a woman and kissing her on the mouth.

I unlocked the outside door, climbed the stairs to our place, hearing Mitch playing something slow and dreary on his saxophone. Maybe I hadn't seen him kissing that woman, but just imagined it. Or it had been somebody else completely, someone resembling Ashanti's father. I toyed with those theories, hoping one or the other would grow into something convincing.

"Hi," I called, entering our apartment. "I'm home."

"Hi," my mom called from the kitchen.

I went in, taking off my jacket, my mind elsewhere. But not a good time for my mind to be elsewhere. Sitting with my mom at the kitchen table, her red leather jacket thrown over the back of a chair, was Dina DeNunzio. My heart started pounding so hard it must have been audible to everyone.

"Robbie," my mom said, "this is Dina DeNunzio—she's a TV reporter. Dina, my daughter, Robbie."

I thought I caught a flash of something brightening Dina DeNunzio's eyes, something like triumph, but if I did, it was gone in no time, and she had her hand to her chest. "My goodness," she said. "Aren't you the girl I ran into the other night at Your Thai? Helping that lovely Mr. Nok with his notice?"

Triumph because she hadn't been sure it was going to be me coming up those stairs? Triumph because she'd succeeded in tracking me down, right into my own home? I had no time to think all that through. "Uh, yeah, I guess so," I said.

My mom looked at Dina, then at me. "Notice?" she said.

"Yeah." What had she told Dina about me? What had Dina told her? How had she gotten my mom to let her in? Questions piled on questions. "Mr. Nok needed a little help in English with this notice he was putting up."

"You never told me," my mom said.

"It was no big deal. Just, you know, a notice on the wall kind of thing."

"A notice about what?" my mom said.

My mom was just being my mom: curious by nature, interested in my life, and a total expert in following a chain of questions all the way to the last answer. I knew that, but still felt annoyed because of the look on Dina's face: she was enjoying watching my mom do her work for her.

"Thanking the customers," I said. "For being, like, good customers."

"Wasn't it a little more than that, Robbie?" Dina said. She turned to my mom. "Coincidentally enough, it relates to what we were just talking about."

"The layoffs?" my mom said.

"Not directly," said Dina. "At least not as far as I know. But Mr. Nok's notice is connected to the failure of the New Brooklyn Redevelopment Project. It turns out he was one of the tenants being forced out."

"I didn't know that," my mom said.

"Of course not," said Dina. "I realize now that wasn't your area."

"I had nothing to do with Sheldon Gunn in any area."

"Right," said Dina. "You mentioned that. Although I can't help wonder where he goes for debt restructuring."

"It wasn't to us," my mom said. "Don't forget he had all that Saudi financing."

Dina laughed. "It's so complicated! What a world, huh, Robbie?"

"Yeah."

"But getting back to something simple," Dina said, "simple and very tangible, it seems that Mr. Nok was also one of the many tenants who had cash shoved through his mail slot the night of the storm. His notice was to thank the anonymous benefactor and offer him—or her—or even them, I suppose—free dining for life."

"So that was true, all those tenants getting money that night?" my mom said. "I heard rumors."

"Me too," Dina said. "That was how I got started on the story."

"What story?" my mom said. "Aren't you working the Jaggers and Tulkinghorn layoffs?"

Dina blinked. Hey, Dina—bet that doesn't happen often, huh? I wanted so much to say that aloud. No way for that, of course. I got the idea that there were two conversations going on here, one audible, the other silent, and that mixing them together would be a big mistake.

"Yes, of course," Dina said. "I misspoke. But they're like opposite sides of the coin."

"What do you mean?" my mom said.

"Just that the NBRP crack-up brought good to some people and bad to others," Dina said.

"What others?" my mom said.

"Why, you and your coworkers, for starters."

"And apart from that?"

"I'm chasing down rumors of related job losses on Wall Street," Dina said. "And maybe in London. But for now, I'd really like to do something on the personal side."

"The personal side?"

"The collateral damage."

"You want to do a story on me?" my mom said.

Dina's glance slid my way, then back to my mom. "Yes, that's the idea."

"I don't consider myself damaged," my mom said. She said it quietly and strongly at the same time. I loved my mom.

Dina smiled. "That's a terrific quote, right there."

"You said this was all off the record," my mom said.

"And it is," said Dina. "Unless you change your mind."

"I won't," my mom said. "And I'm still curious about how you found me, specifically." She looked at me. "Mind checking on Pendleton?"

"Huh?"

"He's upstairs somewhere. Please make sure he's not getting into any mischief."

"He'll just be sleeping, Mom. I—"

"Robbie?" My mom raised her eyebrows. "Thanks, honey."

I turned and went upstairs. This was part of being a kid. You could get sent out of the room on any bogus pretext. I felt Dina's eyes on my back.

"Such a delightful kid," I heard Dina say. "Kind of reminds me of me at the same age. What grade is she in?"

"Seventh."

"I'll bet she's a great student."

"She does all right."

"And where is this?"

"What school?"

"Yes—what kind of school have you picked for such a bright girl?"

Their voices faded.

Pendleton lay on my bed. No surprise. He opened one eye, focused it on me, or close, and shut it, giving a contented little sigh. Did he remember anything of what he'd been like with the charm inside him?

"Pendleton? What do you remember? What did it feel like?"

No answer. No response whatsoever. I went to my computer, checked the temperature: twenty-nine degrees, going down to fourteen overnight. Did they keep it nice and warm in the detention center? Somehow I doubted it.

I went into the bathroom, looked out the front window. Down below, Dina DeNunzio was just coming out of the front door. She walked quickly down the stairs and got in a car. At that moment, I noticed a man sitting in another car across the street. Dina started her car and drove off. The man pulled onto the street. In a cone of streetlamp light, I caught a glimpse of his face. I knew that face, the broad hard face of the man who'd met Sheldon Gunn in the bar at P.O.V.: Mr. Kolnikov. He drove away, following Dina at a safe distance.

• • •

"How was your visit with Ashanti?" my mom said as I came downstairs.

"Uh, good." Which couldn't have been called true, not with Tut-Tut still a prisoner, but where was my starting point when it came to the truth? What I couldn't bring myself to do was take that first step on a long, long road of confession and corrections, with magical stops on the way, a story that would just end up sounding like the biggest lie of all, since I couldn't prove any of it. Did you have to tell your parents about everything in your life? Nobody expected them to tell you, the kid, everything about theirs. But none of that mattered right now. Bottom line: I was trapped in a secret life; a secret life about . . . about being chosen, for whatever reason, to fight injustice. I had to toughen up.

"What, uh, went on with that reporter?" I said.

My mom shook her head. "I really don't know what to make of her. I guess it's a story, these layoffs, but why me?"

"What do you mean?"

"Well, some of the lawyers who got laid off were much more prominent than I am," my mom said. "Those five partners, for example."

"Maybe she's talking to them, too," I said.

My mom shook her head. "Not so far—I e-mailed them all."

"So the story's going to be only about you?"

"I get the feeling she's dropping the whole thing, especially when she realized I wouldn't go on the record."

"On the record means with your name and stuff?"

"Exactly. She wanted to tape an interview. Not too smart to go on TV criticizing your old firm when you're job hunting."

"I guess not," I said. "Um, how's that going, the job hunting?"

"I've got some leads."

"Great. You're an expert, right? Mr. Stinecki—that's the history teacher—says the economy depends on experts more than ever." He also said it was a bad development in terms of human happiness, but I left that out.

Mom looked like she was going to say something pessimistic, maybe undercut her expertise. She held it in, sipped tea from her mug. "Dina was sure taken with you, though."

"Yeah?"

"She said she always wanted children of her own. Seeing you reawoke all that."

Pretty clever, I thought. I said, "So how come she didn't have kids?"

"I didn't ask," my mom said. "I assume it's the same old career-woman story—it didn't work out."

"You're a career woman. It worked out for you."

My mom touched my hand. "No way I was going through life without that," she said.

"Lucky for me."

My mom laughed. Now was the time to hit her with some version of the Tut-Tut story, and I was all set to plunge in, totally unrehearsed, when my dad came in the door, laptop under his arm, face red from the cold.

"What's funny?" he said, taking off his scarf and jacket.

"Nothing," my mom said. "We're just chatting. How was your day?"

My dad shrugged. "Heard from Eleanor Stine—she works with Shep van Slyke's agent."

Agents were important in the book business, and right now my dad was maybe between agents; Shep van Slyke was a writing buddy who sometimes hung out with my dad at Monsieur Señor's.

"That sounds promising," my mom said.

"She's interested in the new book," my dad said.

"Great! So she liked the pages?"

"In general. But there's a catch."

"Oh?"

"There's something else she wants me to tackle first."

"What's that?"

"An assignment, I guess you'd call it."

"A writing assignment?"

My dad nodded. "A paid writing assignment, if that's what you're asking."

"I wasn't," my mom said. "But isn't that good news?"

"Depends on how one sees oneself in life," my dad said.

"I don't follow," my mom said; which made two of us.

"Ever heard of George Gentry?"

"The guy who writes that series about the one-legged detective in Las Vegas?"

My dad looked annoyed. "One-armed detective. But yes, him. He's one of Eleanor's clients."

"That's good," my mom said.

"What's good about it?"

Now my mom started sounding annoyed herself. "Gentry's a big bestseller, isn't he? Therefore Eleanor must be doing well. So it's good she's interested in you."

Kind of strange, since my dad was a writer, meaning a type of communicator, but lots of times I found my mom easier to understand.

"Right now," my dad said, "she's interested in me as a hack. Gentry's overdue on the next book in his series, totally blocked and downing a bottle of scotch a day. He's desperate for someone to write the book for him. The offer's for eighty grand if I can do it in three months."

"Of course you can!" my mom said. All of a sudden

she had some color in her cheeks, looked more like her usual self. "That kind of thing will be a snap for you."

"But you're missing the point!" my dad said. "It's ghostwriting. My name won't even appear. *Dead Man's Hand*—that's the moronic title they've chosen—by George Gentry, even though he won't have written a single word."

Normally I'm not one of those people who thinks about things in terms of numbers. But two numbers arose in my mind right away, and I couldn't get past them: eighty thousand for the dollars; and three for the months of work.

"And after this," my mom said, "Eleanor will take on your new book?"

"She says."

"So I'm missing the downside. You make a nice quick bundle of money and then get back to what you love doing, and with proper representation."

I couldn't have put it better myself, in fact couldn't even have come close. I tried to memorize what my mom had just said, word for word.

Meanwhile, my dad had gone pale. "Hack work, Jane. Hack work. Didn't I make that clear? Is that what you think of me?"

"Three months, Chas, for God's sake," my mom said. Then her voice rose in a way I'd never heard from her. "Do you think I believed in every damn deal I worked on?"

My dad's voice rose, too. "This is different."

"How?" said my mom. "How is it different?"

"I'm an artist, that's how," my dad said. He lowered his voice, lowered his head, too. "There, you made me say it." He turned and hurried upstairs. My mom rose, went into the living room, closed the sliding door behind her. I sat at the table, all mixed up.

13

Ashanti called me bright and early, sounding chipper.

"You sound chipper," I said.

"Uh-oh—did I wake you?"

"Sort of." The truth was I'd been clinging to sleep rather than simply sleeping, in no hurry to rise and face the day. Face things like the sight of Ashanti's dad kissing that woman, something I knew and Ashanti did not. Was it my duty to tell her? Not to tell her? I didn't have a clue.

"What did your mom say?" Ashanti said.

"About what?"

"Come on. Are you in a coma? Tut-Tut, of course."

"I didn't get a chance to bring it up."

I expected some follow-up on that, probably annoyed, but Ashanti let it slide right by. "Doesn't matter," she said. "I've got another idea."

"Like?"

"Silas's dad."

• • •

I went downstairs. No sign of anybody. My mom had left a note on the table. *Good morning, Robbie. I've taken P. for a walk. Back soon.* Under that I wrote, *Gone to the museum with Ashanti. Back later.* A voluntary trip to the museum: I could picture the expression on my mom's face when she considered that one.

Ashanti was waiting for me on the street.

"Hi," she said. "Nice day."

"What's nice about it?" The sky was one big dark cloud, and some strange smell was in the cold air, kind of sewery. "Why are you in such a good mood?"

"It's my natural state."

"Coulda fooled me."

She gazed down at me and shook her head in a tsk-tsk sort of way. "Attitude is everything in life."

"Are you on some kind of dope?" I said.

She laughed. "More like I was a dope."

"Huh?"

"Remember what I told you about my dad? That text?"

"Of course."

"Well, I must've misinterpreted. Not enough data points, as they say in science class."

"What do you mean?"

"Just that my dad's being so nice to my mom lately. They're getting along like I've never seen. They shared a bottle of champagne last night, and he had flowers delivered first thing this morning."

"Oh," I said.

"Oh? Just oh?"

"I meant, that's nice."

"My mom's actually up and having breakfast at this very moment. Granola with banana slices!"

"What's strange about that?"

"She never eats breakfast, hardly eats at all."

I glanced at Ashanti. No sign of the brooding expression that so often lurked beneath the surface of her eyes. She was happy today, plain and simple. So what was I supposed to do with this data point grenade I had in my possession? Keep the pin in, Robbie. If grenades had pins: not my area of expertise. And what if I, too, was misinterpreting? Finding a way through a problem like this: also not my area of expertise. Did I even have an area of expertise, a single one? None came to mind.

My mom was a lover of museums, so I'd visited lots of them, all over the five boroughs, including the Brooklyn Museum, which Ashanti and I entered as soon as the doors opened. We paid the suggested donation for students with valid ID and went up the Arts of the Americas floor, where I'd never been.

"What would Silas do about the suggested donation thing?" I said as we rode the elevator.

"He'd suggest zero," Ashanti said.

We walked past a bunch of Native American exhibits, didn't see Mr. Wilders; there was no one around but a tired-looking security guard pacing her way to the end of the hall and back. We gazed at a picture of a shirtless Plains Indian warrior mounted on his horse. He gazed at something in the far-off distance.

"We ground them up, but good," Ashanti said.

"We?"

"Actually, you. My ancestors were getting ground up, too."

"On your father's side?" I said.

"No," Ashanti said. "Not on my father's side." She took a deep breath, blew it out through her nose. "All this stupid history. What are we supposed to do with it? You can't fix the past. Like basketball—you miss the free throw, and that's that. Play in the now."

We said "play in the now" together. It was a favorite motto of our coach, Ms. Kleinberg, who had a sweet and deadly jumper and had starred for Dartmouth.

"Thatcha!"

"Comin' atcha!"

We high-fived. The security guard came a few steps in our direction, and called, "Help you with something?"

"No, thanks," I said.

We moved away. "I think she missed the irony part," Ashanti said quietly. There were two ways of doing the

Thatcha-comin'-atcha thing, straight up and ironic. Ashanti and I were the ironic types. The kids on the student council did it straight up.

"Does play in the now mean you should actually forget about history?" I said.

"Sounds wrong," said Ashanti.

We came to the Canarsee exhibit. I kind of remembered something about the Canarsees, maybe that they were living in Brooklyn and Manhattan when the Dutch first arrived, and that was how come there's a Canarsie neighborhood in Brooklyn. An explanation on the wall told all about how the Canarsees were part of the broader Lenape people, how they'd eventually sold or traded or lost everything—mostly had it taken away, actually—and how the last survivor was thought to have died around 1830.

We gazed at the glassed-in display of Canarsee artifacts: spears, axes, beaded leather pouches, woven baskets, a drum. And a small stone head, a head with a simple engraved face: two eyes—one round, one a little irregular, a rectangular mouth, a few squiggles for the hair or else for forehead frown lines. Not much in the way of features, but somehow they seemed angry.

And just as I was thinking that, the charm began to come to life. I could feel it warming against my chest, even stirring a bit, as though moving on its own.

"Ashanti?" I said. "Something's happening." I shifted

the charm out from under my shirt and into the open. Ashanti reached out and touched it. For a moment, her face changed, twisting in a way that kind of resembled the angry stone face in the display case.

"Oh, my God," I said.

"What?" she said, and immediately her face went back to normal. Had I imagined the whole thing? "It's warm, yeah," she went on, "but not as hot as it used to get."

"Right, but—"

A door just beyond the glass case opened and out came Jim Wilders—Silas's somewhat wayward dad, as he himself had put it—clipboard in hand, pencil between his teeth. His eyes, so much like Silas's, took in the scene: Ashanti and me by the glass case, the charm out in the open, her finger on it.

"Well, well," he said. "Robbie and Ashanti—we meet again."

"Uh," I said, tucking the charm back under my shirt.

He glanced around. "Where's Silas?"

"At home, probably," Ashanti said.

"For a moment, I thought he'd come to visit me at work—which would have been a first." We had nothing to say to that. He gestured toward the display. "You're interested in the Canarsee people?"

"Kind of," Ashanti said.

"Know much about them?"

Ashanti shrugged. "They used to live here," she said. "In Brooklyn. Then they all died out and—"

"Died out?" said Silas's dad. I noticed his name tag read Professor Wilders. "I guess it depends on what you mean by died out. The fact is there were decades, even centuries, of mixing between native peoples and Europeans, so there's no reason to think Canarsee DNA doesn't live on."

I took a long look at those braids, could feel Ashanti doing the same thing.

"And if their DNA," said Mr. Wilders, "why not some of their ideas and values?"

He paused, glanced at each of us. I didn't know the answer, wasn't sure I even understood the question.

"You're saying ideas and values are in the DNA?" Ashanti said.

Wow! What a smart question! Friends: I knew how to pick 'em. And I could tell from a new expression on Wilders's face that her question sounded smart to him, too.

"I wouldn't go that far," he said.

Ashanti's gaze shifted to his braids. "Do you have Canarsee DNA in you?"

He took a deep breath, let it slowly out. "Not to my knowledge." He got a faraway look in his eyes; at the same time, one of his hands rose slightly and made a fist. Did he even realize it? "Let's just say that ideas and values can live on, especially if we give them a boost."

"How?" said Ashanti.

Mr. Wilders checked his watch. "Got a minute or two? I can show you some of the stuff I'm working on." He opened the door by the display case and ushered us through.

Backstage at the museum, if that was how to put it, the look was standard office building, the characteristic museum smell—sort of airy and marbly—disappearing at once. Wilders led us into his office, a small windowless room coldly lit with strip lights. Books and papers were stacked all over the place and the walls were covered with art—mostly photos of Indians in the old west, but also some movie posters: *Hombre, The Searchers, Little Big Man*. Mr. Wilders went over to one of those stand-up architect tables and cleared a space, revealing a big map of Brooklyn.

"Where do you kids go to school?" he said.

"Thatcher," said Ashanti.

"That's private?" he said.

"Independent," I told him; I liked that description much better.

Mr. Wilders gave me a quick look, like maybe he was changing his mind about me. From what to what? I had no idea. He rolled up his sleeves and turned to the architect table. His arms were sinewy and strong—but what I noticed first was bruising and scrapes around his wrists. He pointed a pencil at the map.

"Thatcher Academy," he said. "Right about here. Not a spot that's come up yet in my research, but that doesn't mean it won't—that's one thing I've learned."

"What research?" Ashanti said.

"See these areas shaded in yellow?" Mr. Wilders said. "Those were all places associated with Canarsee life. For example, here by this bend in the Brooklyn-Queens Expressway, a small village stood for the better part of a century." He pointed the pencil tip down toward the water. "And here on a strand by Gowanus Bay, we've found extensive shell middens."

"Shell middens?" I said.

"Just a kind of dump, really, where the villagers would deposit all their shells. But a totally organic dump, of course, without any negative consequences for the ecology."

"Seashells?" I said.

Mr. Wilders nodded. "Clams and oysters, mostly."

"Oysters?" I said.

"By the tens of thousands. The Canarsees loved oysters, and in those days, you didn't have to pay three or four bucks a pop in some snooty restaurant—you just waded onto the flats and scooped them up to your heart's content." Mr. Wilders got a faraway look in his eyes. "The oysters thrived, what with the water being so pure back then. Is it too much to say that the oysters liked the water they inhabited in precolonial times, even loved it?"

Yeah, I thought it was too much. There was a silence, kind of awkward. I'm one of those people who can't take awkward silences for long. "I hear," I said, "that the oysters are making a comeback."

He faced me, the faraway look fading fast. "Where'd you hear that?"

"Uh, my aunt, actually. My aunt in New Jersey."

"New Jersey," said Mr. Wilders, his voice sharpening. "Is she an expert on shellfish?"

"Maybe not an expert," I said. I didn't want to leave it like that, failing to stand up for my aunt. I liked Aunt Jenna. "But she taught me how to shuck them."

Mr. Wilders's voice lost that edgy thing. "You like oysters?" he said.

"Especially with cocktail sauce."

He turned to Ashanti. "How about you?"

Ashanti made a face. Mr. Wilders laughed. Ashanti and I joined in, a nice, tension-free moment.

"You seem like such good kids," Mr. Wilders said, still chuckling. "So I was wondering what you thought about me getting busted at the Gunn Tower demonstration."

My laughter cut off just like that. "I didn't know what to think," I said.

"I felt bad for Silas," said Ashanti.

Angry red patches appeared on Mr. Wilders's face. "Why feel bad? His father took a stand for something he believes in." He turned and stabbed the map of Brooklyn with his finger.

"See this yellowed-in area? This huge yellowed-in area? That's where Mr. Gunn is lusting to build his tower." He glared at us. "Have you seen pictures of the plans?"

"No."

Mr. Wilders tapped on a keyboard. A picture popped up on a monitor, one of those artist's renderings where the sky is the bluest blue, the grass the greenest green, and the tiny people at the bottom seem full of purpose. Soaring above the tiny people on the screen was a dark tower—the windows dark, the steel dark—that made all of Brooklyn spread out below it seem small and insignificant, merely the setting for the tower, and no more.

"For comparison," Mr. Wilders said, "here's the Empire State Building." Gunn Tower looked to be about twice as tall. "In the early mornings, the shadow will stretch all the way across the borough and onto the East River." I eyed the tiny people. They seemed oblivious to Gunn Tower, like it was just an ordinary tree or something. That didn't strike me as realistic. I could feel the weight of its presence from here.

"Yellowed-in means the Canarsees lived there?" I said.

"Or that it was an important place for them," Mr. Wilders said. "That's the case here. I've established that there was a spring on this site—a stream rising out of the earth—that the Canarsees often drank from and considered sacred. It was also possibly a burial site—the gold standard for stopping development, if provable."

"Where's the spring now?" Ashanti said.

"Gone," said Mr. Wilders.

"How can a spring be gone?" I said.

"A mere spring?" said Mr. Wilders. "That's easy. The whole Colorado River's practically gone. From what I've been able to discover, this particular Canarsee spring disappeared over two hundred and fifty years ago."

"Disappeared where?" Ashanti said.

Mr. Wilders shrugged. "Dammed-up, filled in, diverted—who knows? Lost and gone, one of those losses you can't put a dollar value on, no matter how many casinos get built on native land."

I didn't quite follow the casino part, but the mention of dollars reminded me of something. "Is it true the Indians sold Manhattan for twenty-four dollars?"

"Sixty guilders in trade goods," said Mr. Wilders. "Which works out to about twenty-four dollars at the time. But the point is—what did the Indians think they were trading? Certainly not exclusive rights to the land, because they didn't think of land that way, as something to be owned."

"What kind of trade goods?" Ashanti said.

"Probably some useful things—iron tools and textiles. Plus some decorative objects that you call trinkets if you're trying to make the natives seem like suckers, but that I prefer to call jewelry."

"Jewelry?" I said.

"No gold or diamonds, but nice things, just the same—Italian glass beads, the odd silver charm or two."

"Silver charm?" Ashanti and I both said at once.

He shrugged. "Small. Nothing fancy. Not unlike Robbie's charm—the one you two seemed to be admiring when I came out."

My heart did a little stutter step.

"In fact," Mr. Wilders went on, "I wouldn't mind taking a quick picture of it."

"You—you want to take a picture of . . ."

"If you don't mind," Mr. Wilders said. "I'm getting some visuals together on old trading goods."

"Robbie's charm isn't old," Ashanti said.

"Granted, but it has the look I'm after."

Pause. A pause that got longer. What was there to do but hand it over? I handed it over.

Wilders hefted the charm on his palm, gazed at it

with interest, and then with a lot more interest. "Where did you get this?"

"Um," I said.

"Wasn't it a gift?" said Ashanti.

"Yeah. A gift."

Mr. Wilders gave us a look. "And a very nice one. I suspect it is old, after all. Seventeenth or even sixteenth century, and also European, quite possibly Dutch." He opened a desk drawer, took out a camera, snapped some pictures of the charm. "Who gave it to you?"

"A friend," I said, ready for once with the right kind of answer.

"A very good friend," Mr. Wilders said, giving it back. "Thanks for showing it to me."

"Sure," I said.

"But it's not really why we came to see you," Ashanti said.

"I didn't think so," said Mr. Wilders. "It's about Silas, right?"

"Not really," I said.

"Indirectly," Ashanti added.

"Is he in trouble?"

"No," I said.

Ashanti chipped in again. "Not him."

"I don't understand."

We told him all about Tut-Tut. Not all, exactly, but pretty close, except for the magic.

He listened without a word, his only reaction being a vein that throbbed in his forehead. I realized my mom would have asked a million tough questions; this was better. "I'll see what I can do," Mr. Wilders said when we came to the end. "And, uh, I hope you pass this on to Silas."

"Pass what on?" I said.

"That he's helping," said Ashanti.

Mr. Wilders closed his eyes in an embarrassed sort of way and nodded. Then came a knock on the door. "Jim?" a woman called. "That reporter's here."

"Be right down."

14

We met Silas at HQ. It was cold but not cold enough to see your breath: the space heater, pulled up close to Silas's feet, glowed red.

"Muffins," I said, putting a bag of them on the desk.

Silas opened the bag, poked through. "No icing? I like icing."

"These are healthy," I said. "Blueberry, cranberry, orange, and carrot."

"Carrot cake?" Silas said.

"Maybe."

He took the carrot muffin. "Tut-Tut loves blueberries," he said, taking a big bite. "They don't have them in Haiti," he added—or something like that, hard to tell with his mouth so full.

"Speaking of Tut-Tut," I said, and started in on a description of our visit to the museum.

"Huh?" Silas said, interrupting before I'd barely gotten out of the blocks. "You saw my stupid father?"

"Yeah," I said. "See, we got the idea that—"

"Without even telling me first?"

There was a silence. No comeback occurred to me. I turned to Ashanti. She looked Silas in the eye and said, "You're one hundred percent right."

Silas gazed at her. Seeing her in a totally new way? I was considering that when he shook his head and said, "Can't go that far. One hundred percent represents a degree of certainty you'd never find in situations like this. Call it about ninety-eight percent."

Another silence. And then Ashanti and I were laughing our heads off.

"What?" said Silas. "What's funny?"

We couldn't put it into words, didn't even try. "The point is," I said, "we've got to do something about Tut-Tut, and we thought your father was the type who might help out."

"Because he gets involved with every cause that comes along, even at the cost of neglecting his own family?" Silas said.

"Yeah," said Ashanti, "if you want to put it that way."

Silas nodded. "Makes sense. Did he go for it?"

"He did," I said.

"You left out the charm, of course."

"Not exactly," I said. And we told him about Dutch silver and his father's research into trading beads.

"What does it mean?" Silas said. "Was the charm part of the twenty-four-dollar deal? Selling Manhattan, all that?"

I took off the charm, laid it on the desk. Did it look centuries old? Not that I could see. Nor did it look brand-new. Or in any way magical. But if Wilders was right, the homeless woman who had dropped it had been sitting in front of a once-sacred place.

"Suppose," Ashanti said, "it was part of the deal. Did it have magic properties then, or did it get them as a result?"

"Huh?" said Silas.

"What didn't you understand?" Ashanti said.

"Any of it. I didn't get any of it. Zip, zilch, nada."

"How can anyone be so smart and so dumb at the same time?" Ashanti said.

"The dumb part of me can't tell you," said Silas.

Ashanti blinked a long slow blink, a danger sign. She turned to me. "Do you see what I'm talking about?"

"Uh," I said, "some kind of balancing thing? Making the trade for Manhattan actually more even?"

"Kind of," Ashanti said. "After the fact. More even. More just."

I kind of hoped that the charm might—not hear us, of course, but in some way react, show a little solidarity.

But the charm simply lay there, looking like nothing much. Suddenly it hit me that the wrong person was wearing it. The right person was an orphan, an escaped prisoner, a survivor of a horrible disaster at sea, not someone like me. I'd had a cushy life so far, although when you went to school with kids like Signe Stone, Flagler on her mother's side—cushiest of the cushy—it could slip your mind that you were pretty lucky too.

"Tut-Tut should be the one who wears the charm," I said.

"Nope," they both said at once.

"It chose you," Ashanti said.

"Twice," Silas added. "Homeless woman first and oyster second. And anyway, Tut-Tut's a guy. Guys don't wear jewelry."

"Guys wear jewelry all the time," I said.

"Not guys like me and Tut-Tut," Silas said. "Guys who do guy things."

"Such as?" Ashanti said.

Silas dug through a bunch of inner pockets in his Michelin-Man jacket, dumped stuff on the desk: coils of wire, batteries, electronic components I didn't know the names for, balled-up gum wrappers, a small flashlight, cigarette filter tips.

"Whoa," I said. "You're smoking?"

"Of course not," said Silas. "Checked the stats? These are for an experiment."

"What experiment?" Ashanti said.

"Never mind. It didn't work out." He did some more rummaging. "Here we go." He laid a sort of card on the desk, a small complicated-looking card with blues and greens merging into each other, lots of different-sized writing; and Tut-Tut's picture. "Ta-da," Silas said. "Guy thing extraordinaire."

"What's this?" said Ashanti.

But I knew: Uncle Jean-Claude had one just like it. "A green card," I said.

"Meaning Tut-Tut's legal?" Ashanti said.

"We just have to put this in his hands," said Silas.

"Where did you get it?" I said.

"Get it?" said Silas. "I made it, of course, and it wasn't easy. You're looking at state-of-the-art personal identification, brothers and sisters."

"You made it?" I said. "How?"

"I could explain, but you wouldn't understand."

"But it's not real," Ashanti said.

"Depends on your definition," Silas told her.

"And even if we get it to him, what then?" she went on.

"I can't do all the thinking," Silas said.

We ate muffins. I hung the charm back around my neck. It felt heavy, like it was dragging me down.

"Ahm indereted in dis bring," Silas said.

"No one ever told you not to talk with your mouth full?" Ashanti said.

Silas finished chewing. "I'm interested in this spring."

We hung out across the street from the Gunn Tower construction site. There were no demonstrators around, just normal traffic and some pedestrians, all of them walking quickly, their clothes flapping in the cold wind and everybody looking miserable, like a raggedy army coming and going. The scaffolding in front of the construction site seemed higher than before, and a huge yellow crane now rose over the plywood walls.

"Crane's not moving," Silas said. "Ergo—"

"We told you," Ashanti said. "No more ergos."

"They're not working today."

"Good," I said. "Perfect time to scope things out." Then, like a well-trained, careful kid, I looked both ways before stepping off the curb, and as I did, caught sight of something in a store window that stopped me right there.

It was one of those electronics stores where everything's always loud and aggressive inside. In the window hung a big TV monitor, and on the screen, with the museum as a backdrop, Dina DeNunzio was interviewing Jim Wilders. *Jim? That reporter's here.* Was there a law that I had to be so slow on the uptake?

"Hey!" I said. Everyone looked. We moved almost like one person toward the window. Sound came faintly through the glass.

"But," Dina was saying, "a three-judge panel has ruled that you failed to present convincing evidence of Native American occupation on the site."

"That's their problem," Wilders said.

"Care to explain what you mean by that?" Dina asked.

"Their minds were made up from the get-go."

"Are you questioning the integrity of the judges?"

Wilders looked at Dina with irritation. Then he put his hand on the microphone grip, pulled it closer to him. Dina tried to pull it back. Mr. Wilders stared right into the camera, glared at the whole world. "This is only the beginning of a long, long fight. This city, this country, this planet—they have value far beyond the dollars and cents so beloved by Sheldon Gunn, the mayor, and all their kind." He raised a fist. "Justice!"

Dina, now pretty irritated herself, took back the microphone with a jerk. "Live from Brooklyn, Dina DeNunzio. Back to you, Clint."

A blow-dried silvery-haired guy appeared on the screen, looked like he was searching for something funny to say.

"Is he a bit crazy?" Ashanti said.

"The studio dude?" said Silas. "They're all like that."

"I'm talking about your father," said Ashanti. Her eyes narrowed. "And I thought you didn't even have a TV."

"You've caught me in a seeming inaccuracy," Silas said.

They bickered some more, like one of those old married sitcom couples. I wasn't really paying attention. Instead I was trying to imagine what this part of Brooklyn looked like back in the times Wilders was studying. Now it was big city to the max, with hardly a tree in sight and no grass whatsoever. A stream had come bubbling out of the ground right across the street from us? It was hard to picture.

The light turned green. "Let's go," I said. We crossed the street, cut through a bunch of pedestrians, all of them on phones, talking and texting and not even seeing us, and followed the plywood scaffolding wall on the other side until we came to some holes cut in it for people to see. I stood on my tiptoes and peered through one, seeing a huge pit, much wider than I'd expected, roughly the size and shape of a football field, maybe bigger, and also much deeper. The base of the crane was way, way down there, set deep in the mud. At first nothing moved at all. Then, from out of the sky, a seagull, pure white and very big, came circling down. It swept low over the mud, snatched up a scrap of paper, maybe a fast food wrapper, flapped its wings, and flew away. I remembered seagulls—including a real big one like this—on our wild night at sea, the night I'd lost the charm, and wouldn't have been surprised if the charm had now started heating up or given some other signal. No signal came. Despite that, I made a sort of mental leap on my own. "Suppose we go down there," I said.

"What for?" Silas said. "There's no sign of a spring—I've seen enough."

"I haven't," said Ashanti.

"Two to one," I said.

"So what?" said Silas. "Everybody thought the charge of the light brigade was a good idea, too—until it happened."

I wasn't sure what the charge of the light brigade was, didn't want to get into it. No need to. Ashanti had already moved off, was following the plywood wall. We followed her—Silas in the rear, humming some sort of tune, possibly the kind played for cavalry charges. We came to the next block, turned the corner. This street wasn't as busy. Up ahead, Ashanti had stopped and was bent down, examining where the scaffolding wall met the sidewalk pavement. Was the plywood a little cracked, like maybe something had banged into it? She glanced around. No one to see but us outlaws. She gave the base of the wall a quick, hard kick, knocking out a piece of plywood in one try.

Silas and I approached the opening. Not a big

opening, but just enough room for three kids to squeeze through one at a time.

"No way," Silas said. "I'll never fit."

"You'll have to take off that stupid jacket," Ashanti said.

"I'll freeze to death."

"We'll pass it through, for God's sake!" Ashanti said. "You can put it on when we're inside!"

"Sounds iffy," Silas said.

15

I checked up and down the street. It was one of those city street moments, always brief, when no one was in sight.

"Quick," I said.

Ashanti got down and squirmed through the hole in a flash.

"Silas?"

He unzipped his jacket, started taking it off, got all tangled up, and suddenly the contents of his pockets came spilling out: the coils of wire, batteries, electronic components, balled-up gum wrappers, flashlight, cigarette filter tips, plus lots of other miscellaneous stuff I didn't bother to catalog.

"You're completely unbelievable," I said, kneeling down, scooping up everything, stuffing it all back in the Michelin-Man jacket.

"I'll take that as a compliment," Silas said, making no move to help.

I rolled up the jacket, stuffed it through the hole.

"Hey!" Silas said as his jacket disappeared from view.

"Go!"

He got down, crawled through the hole on all fours, groaning and grumbling. I took one last backward glance, saw a long black car nosing around the corner, darted through the hole.

On the other side, Ashanti was already making her way down the steep earthen slope, switchbacking in long descending diagonals, looking surprisingly small. Silas planted his feet. "No way."

"Come on," I said, tossing him the jacket. "It'll be like snowboarding."

"Which I've never had the slightest desire to do." Silas zipped up his jacket to the very top. Outside, I heard a car purring by, very slow.

"I bet you have a great sense of balance," I said.

"How much?"

I grabbed his hand and tugged him toward the edge of the slope.

"Five bucks?" he said

"All right."

"Might as well pay me now."

We made our way down. The earth was kind of frozen mud, with big rocks sticking out here and there. Silas slipped right away. I caught him before he fell.

"Fork it over," he said, or something like that: hard

to tell through all his huffing and puffing. He went rigid, like he wouldn't take one more step. Then his eyes shifted. He stared at the dug-out sides of the slope. I noticed it was layered like a cake, with thick bands, some almost black, some reddish, some shot through with yellow.

"Interesting," Silas said, and slowly started down, examining the layers as he went, paying no attention to his actual movements, yet not slipping once. At one point, he even leaned out over a rock, scraped up a bit of red-yellow dirt, and tasted it. When we got to the bottom, I held out my hand.

"I'll settle up next time I get my allowance," he said.

"Your mother doesn't give you an allowance."

"Maybe that will change."

We caught up with Ashanti, walked across the bottom of the pit, around the crane and toward the other side. The mud wasn't as frozen at the bottom, glistening here and there in a slippery sort of way, a very darkish sort of mud—I'd never seen mud quite like it. We reached the far side of the pit and stopped.

"What are we looking for?" Ashanti said.

"Bones would be good," said Silas.

I hadn't thought of it so bluntly, but yes, bones were on the list of things that would help prove that Wilders was right. Beads or spear points would have been my preference, but they weren't around either. All there was to see was mud.

"What if we dug deeper?" I said.

"Look how far they've dug already," Ashanti pointed out.

We all raised our eyes to the sky. From where we were, it seemed kind of small—a weird thing to think about the sky—and the distance back to the surface looked huge. I got hit by whatever the opposite of the fear of heights was—fear of depths, I guess—and had to keep myself from scrambling up the slope in panic. A strange quiet swept over us.

"Getting buried alive would suck," Silas said. "The earth would cover your eyes and fill up your nose and mouth, and you wouldn't be able to move a muscle, but you'd still be alive for a minute or two."

"Zip it," Ashanti said.

"Also," Silas went on, as though she hadn't spoken, "see that huge rock up there?" We gazed up at a boulder half sticking out of the mud wall high overhead. "Probably brought here by glaciers in the last ice age, but that's not the point. The point is that with all this rain, an unstable sort of—"

What was this? The boulder was starting to wobble?

"Silas? Are you doing this?"

"Me? How?"

Good question. We seemed to be out of magic at the moment. The charm lay cold against my skin. Meanwhile the boulder wobbled some more, and then with a deep sucking sound, it popped loose and started bounding down. *Thud thud thud*—it bounced against the slope in long curves, rolling massively through the air, straight at us.

"Run!" I shouted. But there was no time. The rock came hurtling right toward us, appearing to grow in size until there was nothing else to see. Then, at the last instant, it struck the edge of a sort of shelf jutting from the slope, and flew right over our heads, before landing on the floor of the pit with an enormous, mud-splashing boom. It bounced one last time and came to rest. And there, just feet from us, where the mud had gotten splashed away, was a shallow depression in the floor of the pit, maybe a foot deep.

"My jacket's all muddy," Silas said.

I knelt down for a closer look at this depression. At the bottom I saw a freshly exposed small wooden square with a wooden ring at one end, everything crusted with mud. I reached down and started scraping the mud away. And as I did, a carved face came into view, a face very similar to the one in Professor Wilders's glass case.

"That ring," Ashanti said. "Could it be a handle?"

"Maybe."

"Making this a trapdoor?"

"I don't know."

"Only one way to find out," Ashanti said.

"Personally," said Silas, "I'm not desperate to know. Plus it's getting cold, and I've got to clean off this mud before my mom—"

Ashanti gave him a look, and he went silent, although it was a snap to imagine him going on about his mom, his jacket, Thaddeus's rehab, chunky peanut butter, red-shift, and the age of the universe. I knelt, got a grip on the wooden ring, and pulled.

Yes, a trapdoor, although it wasn't hinged to anything. The whole wooden square came free, revealing a hole in the ground maybe six feet deep. On three sides, the hole was surrounded by earth, but the fourth seemed to be open. I felt the upward flow of warm, moist air on my face.

"A tunnel?" I said.

"Only one way to find out," Ashanti said.

"Stop saying that," Silas said. "Why rush into anything? What if someone sees us?"

We scanned the walls of the pit, the unmanned crane, the scaffolding rising high over street level. No human being in sight.

"And if it is a tunnel," Silas pressed on, "it'll be dark. How are we going to see anything?"

"With the aid of your trusty flashlight," Ashanti said.

"What if I don't have it on me?" said Silas.

"Then you wouldn't be you." Ashanti held out her hand. Silas gave her the flashlight. She switched it on, shone the light into the hole. The floor was hard-packed dirt. She swept the beam back and forth, then stopped. There, in the circle of light, was a footprint; just one single print of a bare foot, toes pointed toward the tunnel, if in fact it was a tunnel.

"You think someone's down there?" Ashanti said.

"No way," said Silas. "This has all been buried for ages."

"Meaning that's a footprint from long ago?" said Ashanti.

"Logical conclusion," Silas said.

"What else have you figured out?" I said.

"Nothing definitive."

"Share."

"Too soon," Silas said. "And sharing's not my reset position."

"I'm going to smack you," I said—not nice, I know, although I always got a bit charged hearing Ashanti say it to him.

Ashanti went in first, hanging by the edge and then dropping down. I turned to Silas. "You're up."

"I like being last."

"Some other time."

Silas crouched, wriggled around, and lowered himself over the edge, clinging to the surface with his hands.

"Just let go," Ashanti called up. "It's not far."

"It feels far."

"I managed," Ashanti said.

"Does everything have to be a competition?" Silas said. "Oh, my God—I'm slipping." He lost his grip and dropped down, landing with a thud. "Ow," he called out.

"You all right?" I said.

"Scale of one to ten? Three."

"Could be worse," I said, dropping down into the hole and sticking my landing smoothly, gymnastics-style. "Let's explore."

"Or not," Silas said.

Ashanti shone the light into the tunnel—yes, a tunnel for sure, stretching away into murky gloom.

"Don't know about you," Silas said, rubbing his hands together the way people do after a job well done, "but I've seen enough."

We headed into the tunnel, Ashanti first, with the light, then Silas, then me. The walls, floor, and ceiling were all hard-packed dirt. After just a few steps, we came to what looked like the roots of a big tree sticking out of the right-hand wall.

"Hmmm," said Silas. "Member of the oak family, not much doubt about that. The tree itself being long gone, of course."

"Kind of a metaphor," Ashanti said.

"For what?" said Silas.

Ashanti ran her fingers over the twisted root ends. "How come it's warm in here?" she said.

"The earth's got a molten iron core," Silas said. "It's really one big magnet."

"You're saying we're closer to the core of the earth?" I said.

"A little."

"Enough to make it warmer?"

"Just a theory," said Silas.

We moved farther along the tunnel, all eyes on the point where the end of the flashlight beam dissolved into shadow. I saw the tail of a worm poke through the ceiling and wriggle around, as though trying to figure out what to make of this space, just like us.

"What's that sound?" Ashanti said.

We stopped and listened. At first I heard nothing, and then—

"Water," Silas said. "Running water."

"The spring?" I said.

No one answered. We kept going, the sound of running water growing louder. Then, maybe after we'd gone fifty feet or so—my sense of distance didn't seem to work well down in the tunnel—the sound went fainter. We stopped. Ashanti turned back, patting her hand along the wall. Then she began scratching at it.

"A cave-in right now wouldn't be good," Silas said, his voice much quieter than normal.

"Hold the light for me," Ashanti said.

I held the light. She scraped away at the wall. Dirt fell to the floor in little clumps, damper the deeper Ashanti got. When she'd dug a strip maybe a foot long and three inches deep, she motioned us closer.

I leaned in with the light. Ashanti had exposed something rusty.

"What's that?" I said.

"A pipe," said Silas. He ran his fingernail along it; flakes of rust fell to the ground. "A real old one." We could hear running water in it, very clearly. Silas scraped out more dirt and now we could see the rounded curve of the pipe. "Judging by this segment, I'd say it's a pretty big pipe," Silas said. "Maybe three feet in diameter."

"Meaning how big around?" I said.

"Just use the formula," Silas told me.

"That doesn't come till eighth grade," Ashanti said.

"Is that my fault?" said Silas. "I'm in zero grade—why do I know?"

I was on the point of finding the primo sarcastic retort when I felt a soft vibration under my feet.

"What's going on?" I said.

"An earthquake?" said Ashanti.

"That would be rare to the vanishing point in this particular—" Silas began, cutting himself off as the vibration grew, spread to the walls and ceiling, although it was strongest under the floor, and now came a rumble, growing louder. Dirt got shaken loose from the ceiling, as well as little pebbles, and rained down on us. I felt something moving in my hair. The worm! "Gah!" I cried, or some frightened nonword like that, and swept the slimy thing away with my hand.

But no one could have heard me, the rumble now so loud. We clung to each other, the flashlight beam sweeping around wildly, our whole world shaking. The rumble built to a roar, then steadied and began to lessen, fading and fading. The tunnel grew steady again, and the dirt rain stopped falling. It grew very quiet, seemingly quieter than before, nothing to hear but the water flowing in the pipe and our own breathing.

"The train," Silas said. "There must be a subway line right under our feet."

One thing for sure, and that I'd never considered: a lot went on underground. "What about the pipe?" I said. "Is that how they diverted the spring?"

"Makes sense," said Silas. "I wouldn't be surprised if it comes out under the East River somewhere, or maybe in the harbor."

I shone the light around: at the carpet of loose dirt now coating the floor; at the section of rusty pipe, where a thin trickle of water, almost nothing at all, had appeared, unless I'd missed it before; and down along the tunnel, where light got swallowed up by dark.

"So, that'll do it, right?" said Silas. "We've had a nice recon, and what goes down better after a nice recon than a steaming cup of hot chocolate?"

"Don't you want to see what else is down here?" I asked him.

"Not desperately."

"Then go back up and wait," Ashanti said.

Silas rocked back and forth on his heels, like he was considering it.

"Nah," I said. "Silas doesn't want to do that."

"I don't?"

"Not deep down."

Silas thought about that. "Maybe I'll hang around a bit longer."

We started down the tunnel.

"Meaning three or four minutes," added Silas, trailing behind me. "Tops."

The sound of running water faded as we moved away from the pipe. At the same time, the tunnel narrowed—not just the walls, but the ceiling, too, sloping lower and lower. We all had to crouch, and were at the point of getting down on all fours when something whitish gleamed at the end of our cone of light.

"What is that?" I said.

"I don't know," said Ashanti, stopping so abruptly I bumped into her. I felt her fear, and I didn't know anyone more fearless than Ashanti. Her fear spread to me and became my own. But then the truth hit me. I moved forward, my shadow falling on the whitish things.

"This is the proof Mr. Wilders needs," I said.

The others came up and joined me. In a shallow, squarish pit, lay three skeletons, a big one, a slightly less big one, and a small one. The two big skeletons lay on their sides, facing each other—if you could say facing when talking about skulls—and the small one lay on its back in between. Rotten bits of animal skin clothing—leggings, moccasins—were scattered around, and there was also a beaded neck pouch not unlike those in the glass case at the museum.

We stared down. After a while, the little grouping, lit by the slightly unsteady light, lost its power to shock.

"See that?" Silas said, pointing to the biggest skull. "That's a bullet hole."

The shock came back again and hit me full force.

Silas knelt and felt around. "I bet if I— Yes!" He grabbed something, held it on his palm. We leaned in.

"What's that?" I said.

"A musket ball," Silas said.

"Ball?" said Ashanti. "It's not very round."

"That's because it's made of lead," Silas said. "Real soft, so it would get flattened by impact with something hard. Like bone."

I turned to the . . . what to call them? Little family?

That was what sprang to mind, maybe on account of the resemblance to my own family: dad, mom, kid. The basic model. A hole in the head, not much bigger than an M&M—that was all it took. I thought of Tut-Tut, all that remained from his basic model.

Meanwhile I was shining the light deeper down the tunnel. It seemed to come to an end just a few feet past the skeletons, a good thing, because I didn't like the idea of stepping over them, and there was no room to go around.

"Why not call him right now?" Ashanti said.

I took out my phone. No service.

"Then let's—" I began, but then the ground started vibrating again as another train came rumbling through, now more beside us than below us, and even closer. It shook the little family in a way I didn't like seeing at all, and clicked and clacked their bones.

"Five bucks says the wall of the station is less than a foot away," Silas said.

"You don't have five bucks," said Ashanti. "We've established that already."

We retraced our steps, returning to the hole in the ground that had been topped by the wooden cover.

"Here's a problem," Silas said.

No doubt about that: the lip we'd hung from was out of reach.

"You'll have to boost us up," Ashanti said.

"Try your levitating thing," Silas said.

"It won't work," Ashanti said. I knew she was right from the cold feel of the charm, refusing to pitch in. "What's going on with it, anyway?" Ashanti went on. "Why can't we have some normal magic? How much injustice does it need?"

None of us had an answer.

Silas boosted Ashanti up, and then me, grunting both times way more than necessary. She and I leaned down, each grabbing one of his upraised hands, and pulled him up. We replaced the trapdoor and spread dirt over it, filling in the depression, and then stamped around to make everything appear undisturbed, probably not a worry, because snow had started to fall.

"Yes!" said Silas, checking his cell phone. "How will we find the exact spot, you're probably asking? Answer—the magic of GPS! Just imagine if all the old explorers had carried this!"

Then there would have been nothing to imagine. I kept that thought to myself.

"Then there would have been nothing to imagine," Ashanti said.

Silas opened his mouth to reply, but maybe couldn't think of anything, and ended up looking a little downcast.

I scanned all around, saw we had the pit to ourselves, no other people but us in sight.

"Time to call your dad," Ashanti told Silas.

"What for?"

"To tell him what we found," Ashanti said. "What else?"

Silas shook his head. "You do it."

Ashanti gave Silas a look and called the museum; Mr. Wilders had gone for the day. She asked for his number, saying it was important, the kind of follow-up request I wouldn't have had the nerve to make. The woman on the other end took Ashanti's number instead and said she'd pass it on to the professor. Then there was nothing to do but zigzag our way back up the slope of the pit, headed for the gap under the fence. The snow made it even slipperier now, so sometimes we had to use our hands. After a while, I looked up and saw we had far to go. I also thought I saw a pair of eyes watching through one of the observation slots. When I checked again, the slot was empty.

16

This is working out," Ashanti said.

"Yeah?" I said. "Like how?"

We'd parted with Silas—on his way to his apartment, rent-controlled but it also had a doorman—and were walking down our own street, close to home.

Ashanti shrugged. "We did our part. Wilders can take over now."

That sounded right to me and led to another thought. "Maybe we should give him the charm."

"Why?"

"To help him."

Ashanti shook her head. "We've been through this—the charm picked you."

"How come?" I said. "Just because I gave that old lady some change a couple of times? Probably not even two dollars, all together?"

"What makes you think it's the amount that matters?" Ashanti said.

"Come on," I said. "Let's not get crazy."

"Way too late for that, girl," Ashanti said.

We laughed, and were still laughing when we reached Ashanti's stoop. Her front door opened, and her dad came out, zipping up his jacket and moving the way people do when they're in a hurry.

"Hey, Ashanti," he said. "How're you doing?"

"Good, Dad."

"Excellent. Hi, uh, Robbie. You guys look like you've been having fun. Gonna let an old guy in on the joke?"

Ashanti's dad didn't appear the least bit old, actually looked even more handsome than before, his square-jawed face marred only by a fresh but tiny shaving cut under the chin.

"We were just goofing around," Ashanti said.

"Why not? You're on vacation. Coming inside, Robbie? Totally welcome, of course. Just so you both know, Ashanti's mom's napping right now, in case you planned to turn it up to eleven."

"Oh, Dad," Ashanti said, "you're hopeless."

"I'm headed home anyway," I said.

"Nice seeing you," Ashanti's father said. He turned to her. "I won't be more than a couple of hours. Anything special you want me to bring back for dinner?"

"Something warm," Ashanti said.

"Done," her father said; he hurried off, one of those

real fast walkers. I glanced at Ashanti, almost said something.

"What?" she said.

"Nothing."

Dad was at the kitchen table, a stack of books in front of him.

"Hi, Dad."

"Hi." He rubbed his eyes. "Did you see Jane out there?"

"No."

"She's taking Pendleton for another walk—three today, so far."

More than usual? Was that the point?

"Dickens was a great walker," my dad said.

"The *Christmas Carol* guy?"

"Yeah. He walked for miles and miles, thinking up his stories."

"Mom's thinking up a story?"

"Thinking, anyway," he said. "But I'm the one who's supposed to be coming up with a story." He nodded toward the stack of books. I checked the writing on the spines. They were all by George Gentry, the guy behind the eighty-grand ghostwriting gig, and had titles like: *Scorched Earth, Blood Feud, False Witness.*

"You're taking the job, Dad?"

"Haven't decided." He made a backhand gesture at

the books, full of contempt. "I've been reading up, if reading is the word for force-marching your eyes through miles of lifeless print."

"So you don't like it?"

My dad gave me a quick look to see if I was making fun of him, and seemed to decide that I wasn't. "His method is to pile one cliché on top of another till he reaches a hundred thousand words."

"Meaning your job will be easy?"

Now he gave me another look, much longer. Then his expression changed, and he started laughing. He laughed and laughed. Tears rolled down his face—that's a cliché, yes, but I couldn't think of another way to put it. Uh-oh. Did tears from laughter count as crying? I'd never seen my dad cry before; I started to get uneasy.

He wiped his eyes on the back of his sleeve, chuckled a few last chuckles. "You're a great kid—know that?"

"What did I do?"

He didn't answer, just gave me a big smile.

I picked up the top book in the stack, which happened to be *Dead Man's Tale.* On the front was a brightly colored picture of a pair of dice lying in a pool of blood.

"It's about a one-armed detective in Las Vegas?" I said.

"And guess what?" my dad said. "He's right-handed, and the arm he lost in Iraq was his left one."

"I don't understand. That's good, right?"

"For the imaginary detective, maybe," my dad said. "But not for the story. For the story, you have to push things farther than that. How much more interesting to see the bad arm forced to learn on the job."

Hey! I'd never heard my dad sound this way, like . . . like an expert.

"And then," he said, "there's the whole problem of what kind of story to put the stupid guy in, what the mystery's all about." He pointed his chin at George Gentry's books. "They're pretty much all the same—a gorgeous but possibly double-dealing woman gets involved with dangerous Vegas types and the detective steps in." My dad sighed and covered his face. "I'd rather die," he said.

"How about doing something with Native Americans?" I said. The suggestion just popped out, but not exactly from nowhere.

He spread his fingers. Through that sort of screen I saw his eyes slowly lighting up. "Indians in Nevada? Like from one of the ancient tribes? Shoshone, say? And it turns out that the detective—"

"The detective what, Dad?"

But he'd picked up his phone and was punching in a number, didn't seem aware of me at all.

"Eleanor Stine, please," he said, his eyes gazing into some far distance, his intensity something I could feel across the kitchen table. "Eleanor? Chas Forester here.

Please tell George Gentry's people that the answer is yes. I'll take the job."

My mom and Pendleton came home just in time for my dad to invite her out to dinner. She looked so tired and worried, big circles around her eyes, but as my dad told her the George Gentry story—putting me center stage, which felt great, even though I didn't deserve it—her expression changed completely, the circles around her eyes just about vanishing, a transformation that amazed me. Family: yes! For a few moments, I forgot all about my secret life and the problems that came with it.

My mom put on the diamond earrings—the diamonds quite small—that my dad had given her on the publication date for *All But the Shouting,* and they went out.

"Back soon!" They practically ran down the stairs.

I stayed home with Pendleton. He lay down by his water bowl, gazing at me; his normal gaze, not particularly intelligent, maybe not intelligent at all. Still, wasn't he sort of one of the Outlaws of Sherwood Street? I knelt beside him, took off the charm and held it out for him, just to see what happened. He gave it a lick, then lost interest, laying his chin on the floor and exerting zero energy. The charm itself remained unaffected, doing its usual masquerade as a cheap bit of costume jewelry.

"You're not much of a help," I said. "Don't you even

want an update on where we are?" Pendleton's eyes closed. I started in on an update anyway, just to get things straight in my own mind, and was good and tangled up when my phone rang. I checked the screen: Ashanti.

"Hi," I said. "I was just explaining one or two things to Pendle—"

"He called," Ashanti said.

"Mr. Wilders?"

"Who else? I started telling him about the tunnel, and he got real excited."

"Did you tell him about the *C-H-A-R-M*?"

"Not exactly. But I think he suspects something like that. He wants to meet us there."

"When?"

"Now."

"Now? But—"

"It's simple," Ashanti said. "You tell your parents you're going to my place, and I'll tell my mom I'm going to yours."

"Your dad's not home yet?"

"Huh? What's that got to do with anything?"

Yikes. Of all the things I could have said, why that? "Um, my parents went out to dinner."

By total accident, that sounded like it might connect to that stupid question about her dad. Ashanti was silent for a moment, then said, "Leave them a note."

Objections and questions rose in my mind, demanding to be dealt with.

"Come on, Robbie—he's already on his way there."

But not demanding hard enough.

We rode the train, our car empty except for the two of us. Our faces were reflected in the window on the opposite side of the car, vanishing against the white tile walls of the stations, reappearing against the darkness of the tunnels. Maybe it was the harshness of the lighting in the car, but we looked kind of young to me. I recomposed my face, tried to look older. You'd think my stupid glasses would help with that, would have at least that one crummy benefit, but they didn't seem to.

"Did he say anything about Tut-Tut?" I said.

Ashanti shook her head. The train went around the bend, making a kind of scream.

"What about Silas?" I said.

"I called—he's on his way." She took out some gum, offered me a stick. We chewed gum.

"Silas is a pretty cheerful guy," I said. "Considering."

"Considering his weird father, crazy brother, all that?" Ashanti said.

"Yeah."

She blew a bubble. "It's all part of that impervious thing he's got going."

"Impervious meaning?"

"Like the way peer pressure doesn't get to him. My guess is he isn't even aware of it."

"Must be nice," I said.

"Yeah? I'd say the same about you," she said.

"Me?"

"Maybe not."

We laughed. Ashanti gave me one of those punch-taps. I gave her one back. The train slowed down and came to a stop between stations, as sometimes happened, in this case just before ours. We sat.

"I wonder if we're right under those skeletons at this very moment," I said.

"I was thinking the same thing," said Ashanti.

The train started up again and rolled into the station. The doors opened, and we got out. There were cops around, another subway thing that sometimes happened; could have been anything—turnstile jumpers, purse snatchers, out-of-control drunks, kids fighting, adults fighting, a false alarm. None of the cops even looked at us. We hurried up the stairs and out into the cold night.

It was raining again, one of those steady drizzles that misted over everything, including my glasses. We turned left, headed for the Gunn Tower construction site on the next block. A long black car going the other way blew past us, the driver with only one hand on the wheel. He was lighting a cigarette with the other, and the flickering match light illuminated his face and that of his passenger. The driver was Harry Henkel the arsonist, so dangerous to me because he'd seen my face. The passenger was Mr. Kolnikov.

"Did you see that?" I said.

"Yeah," said Ashanti. "What's going on?"

"No clue."

Now there were more police around, some on foot, some in squad cars with their blue lights flashing, plus an ambulance and a TV truck pulling up, all of it blurry to me. I rubbed my glasses on my sleeve, but only made everything blurrier. Without a word between us, we sped up, and soon were running. Bright lights shone on the scaffolding, the fence, the looming tower inside; curtains of mist waved in the night. Down below, across the street and right against the plywood fence, stood a bunch of people, most in some kind of uniform. We were drawn there as though we were getting pulled by a giant magnet, couldn't have stopped ourselves if we'd wanted to. The next thing I knew, we were squeezing through the crowd to the front.

A man lay on the sidewalk, a tall, thin man with long braids: Silas's dad. EMTs knelt beside him, one holding a mask over his face, another messing with some tubes, a third pressing her gloved hand against the side of his head, pressing hard, but that didn't stop the bleeding.

"We're losing him," one of the EMTs said.

"Stay with us, sir! Stay with us!"

Wilders stared straight up, his eyes blank.

"Oh, no," I said. "No."

Silas's dad's eyes shifted, his gaze passing over me, coming back, and stopping: locked right on me. He recognized me, no doubt about it. Under the mask, his lips moved. Mr. Wilders was trying to talk. I could hear the sound of his voice, but I couldn't make out the words.

"Easy, there, sir. Easy. Just stay with us."

But Mr. Wilders didn't want to be easy. He raised a hand to the mask, tried to take it off.

"Not a good idea, sir." An EMT took his hand; Wilders's thumb was bent in an impossible way. "We're going to get you into the ambulance, and—"

At that moment, blood came surging out of Mr. Wilders's nose and mouth. It filled the mask and overflowed. The EMTs crouched closer around him, hands raised as though for action, but no action followed.

"Sir," said one of them, very quietly.

Silas's dad stopped struggling. His eyes, still on me, clouded over and closed. That was when Silas came strolling up.

"Hey, dudes," he said. "What's all the fuss?"

We grabbed him and turned him away, but not fast enough. He saw.

17

My mom rented a minivan—like lots of New Yorkers, we didn't own a car—and drove Ashanti and me upstate to the funeral. The minivan had a TV in back, something about an upgrade, and after a while I switched it on, maybe to push back at all the gloom in the air. Bad idea, it turned out. The first face that appeared on the screen was Dina DeNunzio's.

"Captain Leary, what can you tell us about the cause of death?"

The camera drew back, revealing a police officer with lots of gold on his hat.

"Nothing at this time," Captain Leary said. "We're still awaiting word from the medical examiner."

"Do you suspect foul play?"

"For the moment, we're treating this as an accidental death."

"Accidental?" Dina's tone sharpened, and she thrust the mic closer to the captain's mouth, almost like a jab.

"The subject," said Captain Leary, shooting Dina a quick, cold glare that he might have thought would be just between them but that seemed to happen in slo-mo under the TV lights, clear to anyone, "appears to have fallen while attempting to scale the barrier around the Gunn Tower construction site."

"Scale the barrier?" Dina said. "Were there any witnesses?"

"I can't comment on that at this time."

"Are you aware, Captain, that Professor Wilders was a vocal opponent of the Gunn Tower project and was even arrested at a demonstration within yards of where he eventually met his death?"

"I can't comment on that either. The investigation is ongoing."

"Arrested," Dina pressed on in that relentless way she had (and I was starting to admire it, except when it was aimed at me), "and presumably booked by the NYPD, Captain."

"The investigation, as I said, is ongoing."

"Do you have any concerns about the recent involvement of Russian investors in the Gunn Tower project?"

"I don't see why that would be a matter for the NYPD."

"Some of those Russian oligarchs have a rough-and-ready way of doing business, don't they, Captain?"

"Russia is not my beat," the captain said with a smile, like he'd just scored some points. "My job is to protect and serve the people of New York."

Dina's eyes narrowed. She might have been about to say more, but maybe she heard some cue in her earbud, because she faced the camera and said, "Dina DeNunzio, live at One Police Plaza." Captain Leary was giving her one last glare when the TV people cut back to the studio.

Ashanti and I exchanged a look that meant, *Accidental death? No way.*

"Was that Dina DeNunzio?" my mom called from the front seat. "Talking about Professor Wilders?"

"Yeah."

"No wonder I haven't heard from her—she's got bigger fish to fry."

Was that the reason? I doubted it. Dina had just been using my mom to get to me. I switched off the TV.

This was my first funeral. It was probably different from most funerals, because it didn't take place in a church or any other kind of religious building, but also like them because of the sad speeches and all the crying that went on. Maybe not a whole lot of crying, actually, but some.

We sat in a meeting hall next door to a small casino on Native American land. There were two long rows of benches, nearly every seat filled. My mom, Ashanti, and I were about halfway back on the left-hand side. Silas sat up front on the right, next to a woman with dark curly hair whom I took to be his mom, and an older kid, who looked a lot like her and had to be Thaddeus. Beside them was a space, and on other side of that, all by herself, sat an older woman whose white hair had just the faintest tinge of red in it. She cried the most.

"The worst thing that can happen," my mom whispered to me. "The child dies before the parent."

The speeches were all about the life of Professor Wilders, but concentrating mostly on the importance of his studies to the Native American community and touching hardly at all on his roles as father or husband. There was also some news: a benefactor had started the Jim Wilders Memorial Scholarship to help Native American kids go to NYU. Some applause started up at that announcement, applause that faded fast when the tall guy at the podium, some kind of chief, revealed the name of the benefactor: Sheldon Gunn. A silence fell, and then I thought I heard a grumble or two. The chief raised his hand in a way that seemed to mean "this is no time for pettiness" or maybe simply "be good." The grumbling stopped at once.

"I appreciate your coming," said Silas's mom in the parking lot when it was all over.

"We're so sorry," my mom said.

"Thank you," said Silas's mom. Up close she looked nothing at all like Silas: she was thin and dark, her eyes filled more with worry and anxiety than sorrow, at least in my opinion. She kept glancing at Thaddeus, standing by himself and kicking halfheartedly at a crusty snowbank. Thaddeus had his mother's curly hair, except his hadn't been cut in some time and grew wildly in a huge dark halo.

Ashanti and I stood close to Silas, one on either side. He didn't say much. I squeezed his hand, realizing as I did so that it was balled up tightly inside his mitten. Ashanti leaned over and gave him a quick kiss on the cheek.

My mom dropped us off on our street before returning the car. We stood halfway between our two houses.

"Accidental death?" I said.

"No way," said Ashanti, her eyes hard. "He was going to meet us. Why would he try scaling the fence before he knew what we had to say?"

"Maybe he got impatient." I couldn't think of any other reason.

That remark got me a real irritated look from Ashanti. "But why?" she said, as we came to our block and started down the hill. "We weren't late. And he's—he was—a smart guy."

"What about the scholarship thing? How does that fit in?"

Ashanti was opening her mouth to enlighten me on the so-therefore part, when a woman appeared on the street, coming in our direction. She was tall, walked in a regal way, and wore a dark fur coat, but there was something odd about her. Her feet. Yes. Her feet were bare, and it was much too cold for that.

"Oh, my God," Ashanti said. "Mom?" And then she was running.

My first instinct was to run after her. Then I thought it was none of my business. But resuming my normal pedestrian pace seemed kind of uncaring. Why was everything so complicated? I ended up doing a kind of speed walk.

As I got closer, all the details grew clearer, details like the richness of the fur, most likely mink, which I knew on account of Nonna also having one, although not this glossy; Ashanti's mom's bare feet, so beautifully shaped, the left-foot toenails painted bright red, the right-foot toenails unpainted; and Ashanti's mom's face, probably the most beautiful face I'd ever seen, at least the way she looked on the old framed *Vogue* cover on their living room wall, but now much too thin. And the eyes: so dark and frightened.

Ashanti already had her by the arm. "Mom? What's wrong?"

Her mom looked annoyed. "Nothing's wrong. I'm just getting some fresh air, that's all. I can't stand being cooped up one more minute."

"But—"

"Not one more second! Not even one more whatever's smaller than a second!"

"But Mom!" There were tears in Ashanti's eyes, not something I'd ever seen. "It's cold outside."

"Of course it's cold," her mom said. "Why do you think I resurrected my mink?"

Resurrected her mink? I missed that one, although it still made me uneasy, and I was already plenty uneasy.

"Mom!" Ashanti said. She lowered her voice. "You're in bare feet."

Ashanti's mom gazed down at her feet. The expression in her eyes changed, like she was waking up.

"Where's Dad?" Ashanti said, even softer than before.

"Working," said her mom. "He must be working. He works so hard. I feel guilty."

"Don't feel guilty, Mom," Ashanti said. "Come on—let's get inside."

"Inside is depressing."

"But it's warm."

At that moment, Ashanti's mom appeared to notice me. "Hello, Robbie," she said. "You look very pretty in those glasses—don't let anyone tell you different."

"Uh, thanks," I said, and then stood there kind of

stupidly before blurting out, "but it sure the heck is cold out."

Ashanti's mom studied my face for a moment, then nodded. "You're a clever girl. Ashanti, sweetheart? Let's go home."

Ashanti led her mother to their stoop, giving me one anguished backward glance.

Back at home, Pendleton was lying on my bed, very comfortable. I squeezed in beside him.

"That thing about sorrows coming in battalions—where are you with that?" I said.

Pendleton didn't open his eyes, but did raise his tail slightly and let it thump gently back down. Meaning what? I had no clue. On the other hand, closing my own eyes seemed not only like a good idea, but unstoppable. Pendleton cuddled in closer, or maybe tried to push me off the bed.

My sleep was all about wandering through dark tunnels and dodging cave-ins. Sometime in the middle of the night, I heard Tut-Tut screaming, "Help me! I'm buried alive." My eyes snapped open at that point, and I found that one of Pendleton's floppy ears had flopped right on my face.

"Pendleton!" I gave him an angry shove, moving him about an inch. After that I rolled around sleeplessly until the first gray light of dawn came through my curtains. I got up right away.

"Come on, Pendleton. We're going for a walk."

His eyes remained closed. Somehow, without actually doing anything, he made himself seem heavier, less moveable. I didn't even try. Instead I went into the bathroom and got ready for the day, checking myself in the mirror, glasses on and glasses off. Did I look clever? Not that I could see. I got dressed, went past my parents' silent bedroom and downstairs, slipping on my jacket as I opened the front door.

And closed it, real quick. Because standing right across the street—and checking her watch, a lucky break for me—was Dina DeNunzio.

I stood in the downstairs hall, just breathing. What was Dina doing here? What did she want? It had to be about Mr. Wilders. Had he told her about meeting some kids just before her interview with him? And then she'd seen us at the scene of his death, and thought . . . what, exactly? I tried to ride herd on all the facts, the speculations, the imaginings, and force them into some kind of order, and was getting absolutely nowhere when Mitch the landlord's door opened, and Mitch himself stepped into the hall.

"Uh," he said. "Robbie?"

"Hi," I said.

He rubbed his chin. I hadn't seen Mitch in days, even

though he lived right under us—the kind of thing that might not make much sense to noncity people. Mitch looked terrible, hair all messy, face unshaved for a week or more. Immediately after he'd lost his Wall Street job, I'd heard him playing his saxophone pretty much nonstop, but now I realized the sax had fallen silent.

"Up early?" he said. "If it's early. Feels sort of early."

Uh-oh. Was Mitch on something or other? This wasn't like him at all. He was usually so crisp and decisive.

"I'm going for a walk," I said. "An early walk."

"Me too," he said, gesturing toward the door.

"After you," I said.

He paused, gave me a sort of sideways glance. "What grade are you in, again?"

"Seventh."

"Where?"

"Thatcher."

"Thatcher," he said. "Good school. Not cheap." He licked his lips; his tongue looked dry and crusty. "Think your parents would be interested in buying the place?"

"What place?"

"This." He tapped the wall. "The building where you live. Nothing like home ownership—isn't that the dream?"

"You're selling the building?"

He rubbed his face again, a little too hard. "Everything's on the table," Mitch said.

"I'll, uh, mention it," I said.

"You do that." He opened the door. I backed into the shadows, but as I did, saw that the street, at least the section in view, was empty, no sign now of Dina.

"Well?" said Mitch, holding the door. "Do I look like a doorman?"

For sure not. I went out, checking up and down the street for Dina. Gone. Mitch turned toward the river. I went the other way, would have gone the other way from him, no matter what.

18

Once my dad said—quoting somebody, I think—that in dreams begin responsibilities. I'd had no clue what that meant, but maybe now I was inching toward it, because I found myself headed for the Flatbush Family Detention Center, last night's dream of Tut-Tut buried alive still somehow wakeful in my mind, making me worried and anxious.

A big white bird—maybe a seagull, but what was a seagull doing this far from the shore?—was perched on the tall dark wall of the detention center. As I walked toward the archway, its head turned, as though following my progress. I got more worried and anxious, for no reason I could explain, and was running by the time I reached the archway.

No one to be seen in the yard beyond those double-barred gates.

"Tut-Tut?" I called. "Tut-Tut?"

No response. I laid my hand on the charm, hoping it

would do something. Nada. The charm had lost some of its power, for sure, maybe all; or it just didn't care. But how could it not care about Tut-Tut?

"Tut-Tut!"

My voice came back to me, bouncing off the hard bricks of the inner wall. And what was that white thing lying by the wall's base? Not a . . . ? But yes: a shoe; a sneaker; a laceless sneaker, once mine, then Tut-Tut's, and now?

"Tut-Tut!" I shouted at the top of my lungs.

For a moment, more silence. Then I heard footsteps, the kind hard shoes make, and a man in a green uniform appeared in the yard. He saw me and glared.

"What's all this racket?" he said.

"Where's Tut-Tut?"

"Huh?"

"Tut-Tut. You've got him locked up in here."

"You're talkin' about a detainee?"

"Yeah."

"There's no fraternizing with the detainees."

"What does that mean? I just want to talk to him."

"Why?"

"Because he's my friend." I pointed through the bars. "And that's his shoe over there. Why isn't he wearing it?"

The guard turned slowly and looked back. When he faced me again, his expression wasn't quite so belligerent. "Stuttering kid?" he said.

I nodded. There was way more to Tut-Tut than that, but this wasn't the time.

"They moved him."

"Where?" I thought, *Haiti?* "Where!"

"No need to shout. You got the loudest mouth I ever heard on a kid. He's in the Annex."

"What's that?"

"Smaller facility. He'll be safer there."

"Safer? From what?"

"Some of our customers in here ain't so good at minding their manners."

"Oh, my God—is he hurt?"

"He'll be all right. It's nicer over at the Annex."

"Where is it?"

The guard named a street I knew, not far from the Gunn Tower construction site. "Number one thirty-three."

I took the train, got off at the stop near the site, turned the corner and started down the street the Annex was on. The wind was picking up, blowing sooty particles around, sooty particles that scratched at my face and eyes. I came to number one thirty-three. It was a plain concrete building, three stories, with barred windows and a guard at the front door. On one side of the building stood an apartment building with a convenience store on the ground floor; on the other side there was a narrow alley with a sign reading ABSOLUTELY NO PARKING. I walked down the alley.

At the rear of the building was a yard surrounded on three sides by a fence topped with razor wire. This yard was bare just like the yard at the detention center, featureless pavement with a round drain cover in the middle, and much smaller. No one was in it. I gazed up at the windows on the back wall, none of them barred, probably on account of the fence.

"Tut-Tut! Tut-Tut!"

And all of a sudden there he was, behind one of the windows on the third floor, his face looking so small, and not at all clear through the grimy glass.

"Tut-Tut!" I waved kind of frantically.

He waved back. Then he tried to open the window but it wouldn't budge. His lips moved. I couldn't hear him at all, although just from how his lips were moving I knew that he was stuttering his worst. He went back to waving. We waved at each other. A big form appeared behind Tut-Tut.

"Tut-Tut!"

He got grabbed. I caught a glimpse of some huge guard pulling Tut-Tut away from the window. I waited for maybe ten minutes, and he didn't come back.

I walked away, going nowhere in particular, and after a while, an idea hit me. That was always strange—although it hardly ever happened to me—an idea zooming in from out of nowhere. I went into a store and bought a can of purple spray paint, purple being Tut-Tut's favorite color for tagging.

Not long after that, I was back at the Gunn Tower site. Rain was slanting down now, rain mixed with snowy white streaks, and the air was growing colder. No work seemed to be going on, from what I could see—the crane loomed motionless behind the fence—and the windshields of the cars and trucks going by were all foggy, plus the pedestrians had their heads bowed against the weather. No one had any interest in one lone kid.

I crossed the street. Police tape was still up around the spot where Mr. Wilders had died, and a few bouquets lay on the pavement. I glanced around, stepped under the police tape, aimed the spray paint can at the plywood fence and, in my best imitation of Tut-Tut's style, wrote *Mr. Wilders Lives!!!* Wrote it big and tall. Then—zoom!—what was this? Another idea out of the blue, so soon? Yes! How about adding an image of the Canarsee stone head, the one Ashanti and I had seen in the museum case. Not easy, especially given my low level of artistic talent, but I was all set to take a swing at it when I noticed a long black car idling in front of a deli on the other side of the street. That's a sight you see in the city, limo drivers grabbing a soda and sandwich on the fly, so my gaze swept right over it.

And then, sort of on its own, swept slowly back. The front doors of the limo were opening, and two men were getting out. The driver: Harry Henkel, now wearing a tight little ski hat that made him look more ratlike than ever. The passenger: Mr. Kolnikov, trench coat collar curled up around his thick neck. They saw me, no doubt about it. I took off. They tried to cross the street but got blocked by the traffic, suddenly very heavy.

I'm a pretty fast runner, actually faster since I started playing basketball for the Thatcher seventh-and-eighth-grade team. Ms. Kleinberg's a great coach, covers all the details, including how to run faster. *Claw the ground, don't push at it! No long sloppy strides—shorten up! Head steady! Relax!* I was doing all that right now—except for the relaxing part—as I raced past the main entrance of the construction site, the artist's rendering of a skyscraper-sized Sheldon Gunn showing off his tower looming over me. As I came to the first cross street, I glanced back to see if I was being followed, maybe not the best time for that; at least I probably should have checked the light first.

BLAAW! BLAAW! A bus, coming right at me, honked and honked again. I glimpsed the face of the driver, scared out of her mind and also real mad at me. She swerved. I swerved. More honking came from all around, plus from behind, I heard screaming brakes. And maybe a thud and a cry of pain, but I was too focused on darting through the traffic to be sure. I charged onto the sidewalk across the street, turned right, and sped on, taking one more glance back. And there was Harry Henkel, picking himself up off the street and getting yelled at by a furious driver. He limped back toward the opposite sidewalk. What about Kolnikov? No sign of him at all. Had I lost him? I ran toward the nearest subway station, halfway down the block, still running my hardest, even if I was in the clear. *Claw the ground! Short strides! Head up!* I was steps away when a long black car—*the* long black car—squealed to a stop beside me and Kolnikov jumped out. I practically ran right into him! He was even raising his thick arms to catch me.

I zipped sideways, just like a running back in football, and Kolnikov grabbed nothing but air. As I went past, I saw him close up, especially those eyes, the pale blue of icy winter mornings. "Stop right there," he said, and called me a bad name, but of course I didn't stop. In fact, I got hit by a brainwave: *Why not run back across the street, through all that traffic again? Who would expect that?*

BLAAW! BLAAW! Another bus! More honking, braking, shouting. And me, making all these moves, the fastest, dartingest moves of my whole life. What I didn't take into account was how hard the rain was falling, and also how it had turned mostly to snow, and all of a sudden, right in the middle of the street, I lost my footing and went sliding on the pavement, sliding and sliding with an enormous dump truck bearing down right at me.

BLAAW! BLAAW! Was I going to just slide by, a mere body length or two in front of it? No, not quite—I wasn't going to make it. "Charm! Do something!" I cried that out loud. But no. Not a thing. So what was the point of all this? Was the charm just going to sit there and let me—

The front wheels of the dump truck thundered past, inches from my head. I kept sliding, totally helpless, sliding and sliding and—and right under the truck and out other side, just ahead of the next set of wheels. I popped up on the sidewalk—practically right in the astonished face of a newsstand guy covering his papers with a tarp—and kept going.

I took one last look back. Kolnikov and Henkel were standing by the long black car, having an argument with a meter cop. The meter cop was . . . yes! . . . writing a ticket. I got a lot of satisfaction from that, and was still enjoying the scene when Henkel snatched the ticket and got behind the wheel. But Kolnikov did not join him in the car. Instead he started peering around, his head turning slowly in my direction. I ducked into the doorway of the store right behind me.

"May I help you?"

I turned. The store happened to be one of those

antique places—not the fancy Manhattan type where if, as Nonna liked to say, you had to ask the price then you couldn't afford it, but the funky type my mom was fond of, full of what my dad called junk. There was only one person in the store, a woman clad all in black except for the fox stole around her neck, the kind of fox stole with the fox's head still on it, first time I'd seen one in real life.

"Um," I said, at the same time noticing that the woman's hair was pretty close to the color of the fox, except too bright to be natural. "I'm just sort of . . . uh, looking."

"For anything in particular?" the woman said. The glass eyes of the fox seemed to be watching me suspiciously.

The answer to her question was no: just looking meant looking for nothing in particular. But this woman didn't seem to be playing the game that way, and all I wanted at the moment was to stay off the street, so I blurted the first thing that came to mind.

"How about Canarsee objects?" I said. As I spoke I felt the charm—heating up now at last but when I didn't really need it—*a bit late on the uptake, little guy*—and no doubt for reasons of its own.

"Canarsie objects?" she said. "Like souvenirs from the Canarsie Pier?"

"Do they sell souvenirs?" I said. I didn't remember any of that from my one visit.

"I'm not familiar with that part of Brooklyn," the woman said.

"No problem," I said, getting the idea from her voice that she was from some other part of the country, maybe the Midwest. I myself was Brooklyn born and bred. "I'm actually talking about the Canarsee Indians." The charm warmed up some more, like it was encouraging me. I moved a bit deeper into the shop.

"The Canarsee Indians?" the woman said.

"They lived here first," I told her. "Right here in Brooklyn, before the Europeans. They were actually part of the Lenape people."

"And they made art?"

"Oh, yeah," I said. "The museum has—" I paused. A small TV stood on a shelf in a corner of the store, and I suddenly realized Dina DeNunzio was on the screen. I walked closer. She was wearing her cool red jacket, standing in a hospital lobby and talking to a tall guy in a white coat who was gazing down his nose at her.

"And the cause of death, doctor?" Dina said.

"Blunt-force trauma to the head," said the doctor. "In layman's terms."

"Layman's terms—thanks, doctor," Dina said. "And what was the nature of the blunt-force trauma?"

"Nature of the trauma? Not following you."

"In layman's terms, how did Professor Wilders's skull get bashed in?"

The doctor gave her a disgusted look, like she'd said a bad word. "His injuries are consistent with a fall from a height of ten feet or more onto a concrete sidewalk. I'm told by the investigating officers that the deceased had been attempting to scale a high fence."

"But so far," Dina said, "no eyewitness has come forward to verify that assertion, so it has to remain an assumption, doesn't it?"

"The deceased died of head injuries consistent with a fall," the doctor said.

"But are you sure that's what happened?" Dina said. "Could a blunt force from something other than a fall be the cause of those injuries?"

The doctor opened his mouth, closed it, glanced off camera, as though for help.

"And if not," Dina said, moving in on him, "why not?"

"I can't comment on that," the doctor said.

"So it remains a mystery?"

The doctor's voice rose. "I never said that! It's no mystery."

Dina faced the camera. "Back to the studio."

"What's that all about?" said the storekeeper, standing behind me.

I turned to her and, as I did, glimpsed a man through the shop window: Kolnikov. He was walking quickly by, cell phone to his ear. Meaning he'd lost me, right? Had to be. A sensation of relief swept over me, and with it, kind of as a bonus, came another brainwave: *How about if I followed him? Any reason why not?* I got the nagging feeling there might have been, but there was no time to reason things out.

"Hey, thanks," I said, hurrying to the door.

"Wait! What about the museum? That sounded inter—"

19

Snow now, for sure, but not the soft puffy kind. This snow came angling down on my face in hard and icy pellets. They didn't seem to bother Mr. Kolnikov, striding along half a block in front of me. He was Russian, right? Maybe Russians got so used to snow it stopped affecting them. Kolnikov was the only pedestrian around not bending into the wind, but bearing himself straight and tall, the snow starting to coat his broad shoulders. He turned right at the first corner, disappearing from view. I ran to the corner, reaching it just in time to see him ducking into a restaurant. The sign hanging over the sidewalk read HAPPY'S PLACE.

I slowed down as I went by, glancing through the streaky window. Happy's Place was pretty dark inside, seemed long and narrow with two rows of booths stretching into the gloom. There were a few shadowy customers, but all that stood out was Kolnikov's blond head. He was sitting with his back to the door, not too far from the rear of the restaurant. By the time I'd absorbed all that, I was a few steps beyond Happy's Place. I found myself coming to a halt, then moving, as though not really under my own control, back toward the door. This seemed to be a day for irresistible brainwaves, and besides, the charm was—but no. It had cooled back down, like it hardly had the strength to come alive for more than a minute or two. No time to puzzle that out. I entered the restaurant.

No one gave me a glance. I took in the scene: an old couple sitting silently in a booth to the left, a woman doing a crossword puzzle to the right, some empty booths and then Kolnikov alone in a booth, phone to his ear. At the very back was a swinging door to the kitchen, weak light entering through its small round window. Without any sort of plan in mind, I slipped into the booth right in front of Kolnikov's. The top of his head was just visible over the leather-covered barrier between the booths. And then I thought, *No in here has seen me. It's like I'm not even here! So why not keep slipping on down, Robbie?* Finding no reason not to, that was what I did, easing myself down into a sitting position on the floor. It was nice and dark under the table, although kind of sticky. A half-eaten french fry on the floor glistened dully with ketchup. I realized I was hungry and fought off a crazy urge to eat it. It hit me for the first time that maybe I had something in common with Pendleton, a completely whacked-out thought.

"Hey, Alexei," said Kolnikov, speaking quietly in his phone. And then came a whole lot of talk in Russian. You heard Russian in Brooklyn from time to time—say, if you went down to Brighton Beach for a swim in the summertime—but you had to be prepared for the fact that Russian men and American men have very different ideas on the proper size for a bathing suit. The American way is better; let's leave it at that.

I heard the squeak of the kitchen door opening, and then came footsteps. From where I sat, I could see only the feet and lower legs of the waitress: she wore paint-stained sneakers and black leggings.

"Care to see the lunch menu?" she said.

"I am on phone," said Kolnikov.

A slight pause, and then the waitress said, "I'll just leave it with you, then." And she put the menu on the table; pretty much slapping it down, actually—I heard the sound distinctly. Kolnikov went back to talking in Russian, with a word or two in English sometimes popping up: "money," "tower," "kids."

Whoa. Kids? What was that all about? I strained to listen but no more English words went by. Soon I heard footsteps again, this time coming from the front of the restaurant. Another pair of legs appeared, a man's legs.

His shoes were black leather, rich and gleaming, with a pattern of tiny round holes in the toe caps; I smelled the shoe polish. His pants were deep navy in color, with a faint pinstripe pattern, the fabric dense and almost like something alive.

Kolnikov quickly said something that sounded like "Poka," and clicked off. His seat squeaked, maybe because he'd turned to look up at the newcomer. "Good morning," he said.

The newcomer stepped out of my view, turning to sit opposite Kolnikov in his booth. "What say we skip the pleasantries?" he said in a low voice. "What the hell is going on?" A voice I knew well and would never forget: the voice of Sheldon Gunn.

"To business, then," Kolnikov said, not sounding at all put off by Gunn's rudeness. "The American way. In Russia, we too have our ways."

"I'm aware of that," said Sheldon Gunn. "I'm starting to think they're superior."

Kolnikov laughed. "This remark I will pass on to my principals in Moscow." He stopped laughing, lowered his voice. "And now I come to troublesome professor, handled in the Moscow way."

"No need for me to the know the details, Kolnikov," Gunn said. "As long as your work leaves no traces."

Kolnikov was silent for a moment.

"You're hesitating?" Gunn said.

"Traces are always possible in a world of more than one being," Kolnikov.

"Skip the philosophy," Gunn said. "Are you telling me we have a problem?"

"Skip philosophy is not Russian thought," Kolnikov said. "But no, no problem, exactly. We now have ruling death by accident."

"That's better. Clumsy fellow lost his footing?"

"*Da,*" said Kolnikov. "But we still have potentiality of issue."

"What issue?"

"Is complex," Kolnikov said. "First is research of professor into subject of—"

He broke off. The paint-spattered sneakers and black leggings—all I could see of the waitress—reappeared.

"Hi," she said, her body turned toward Gunn. "A menu?"

"Coffee," Gunn said.

"Dark roast, medium Guatemalan, Ugandan fair trade mountain light, Vienna—?" she began.

"Coffee," Gunn said. "Fresh. Hot."

"For me, espresso," said Kolnikov. "Double."

The waitress spun on her heel and went away; an angry kind of spin. The restaurant experience from down on the floor was a whole new thing.

"Go on," Gunn said.

"Indian research is first issue," Kolnikov said. "Your professor friend—"

"He was no friend of mine."

"Slight joke," Kolnikov said. "Americans are big fans of humor, no?"

"Not this American," said Gunn. "Get back to the research."

Kolnikov was silent for a moment. I was starting to learn that there are many different silences: this was the annoyed kind. Kolnikov cleared his throat, maybe getting rid of the feelings he was holding in.

"The professor was making research into former burial grounds," he said. "Sacred burial grounds, if you understand my meaning."

Gunn banged his fist on the table. "What a totally bogus reason for stopping a project of this magnitude! All these idiot causes end up doing is raising the cost—passed onto the end user, of course."

"Of course."

"So—is there anything to his research?" Gunn said. "Did he have the goods?"

"This is potentiality issue. I do not believe he had goods, but is not sure thing. I am guessing he was in process of searching for goods when I—when unfortunate accident happened."

"I don't believe in guesswork."

"Same with me," Kolnikov said. "We are peas in pod in that respect."

"I wouldn't—" Gunn began, cutting himself off when the waitress reappeared.

She set the drinks on table and said, "Anything else?"

"No," said Gunn.

Not no thank you; just no. Kolnikov made no reply at all. I decided right then that waitressing would be a career path I'd try to avoid. She ripped the check off her pad. It entered my field of view as she laid it, harder than necessary, on the table.

After she'd gone, Gunn said, "I can't depend on guesswork. You're saying it's possible some sort of deal-breaking remnants are buried down there?"

"Is possible."

"Then we have to do something," Gunn said. "Something definitive."

"Definitive is meaning?"

"Settling things once and for all."

Another silence, the thoughtful kind. "Detonation, perhaps?" Kolnikov said after a while.

"Detonation?"

"Deep down under. Speciality of my company, in fact, but all inclusive in price."

"Hmmm," Gunn said. "Deep down under—I like the sound of that."

"No sound," said Kolnikov. "Is beauty of it."

Gunn laughed. I'd never heard him laugh before, wasn't sure at first it was laughter I was hearing now, so harsh and grating. "You are a funny guy," Gunn said.

"Is mutual," Kolnikov told him.

Gunn stopped laughing. "No witnesses," he said. "That's crucial."

"Bringing us to potentiality issue number two," said Kolnikov. "The snooping wretches."

"What snooping wretches are you talking about?"

"These kids."

I went cold.

"Kids?" Gunn said. "What kids?"

I leaned closer, straining my hardest to listen, not to miss a word, a syllable. But Kolnikov said nothing. Why not? The explanation quickly arrived: more footsteps came pattering in from the front door. A man and woman appeared, or rather, the lower halves of them, the man wearing clogs and jeans, the woman in thigh-high leather boots. They stopped at my table and the woman said, "How about here?"

"Sure," the man said.

They started squeezing into the booth: my booth. I was so caught up in avoiding their feet, shifting toward the wall as far as I could, making myself small, that I almost missed the fact that there was something familiar about the man's voice.

Or maybe not. I couldn't be sure. And what about

Gunn and Kolnikov? That was the point. I was missing important stuff, almost certainly about me and the outlaws. I cocked my ear toward the next booth. They no longer seemed to be talking. Why not? Had I already missed Kolnikov's answer? What did he know? It must have been a lot—why else would he have chased me? Speak! But Kolnikov did not speak, at least not loudly enough for me to hear, and neither did Gunn. Instead I heard the scrape of their shoes on the floor, and the next thing I knew, they were on their feet and walking right past my booth. Not shoes in Kolnikov's case: he wore boots, and left muddy tracks, a strange very darkish mud unlike any I'd seen before—except for once.

No time to get into that now. They were leaving the restaurant! Somehow I had to follow them! But how could I get out from under the table without being seen by this couple, and in the resulting fuss Gunn and Kolnikov would turn and see me, and then . . . I didn't know what would happen then, didn't want to know. If I waited till the couple had done eating, Gunn and Kolnikov would be long gone. What about waiting only a minute or two, time enough for them to get outside? Would it matter by then if I drew attention to myself here in the restaurant, shooting out from under the table? What if the restaurant people thought I was some kind of thief? Yikes. It was actually sort of true. All these thoughts were zipping back and forth across my mind when the man sitting in my booth—just a foot or so away, his knee practically in my face—spoke.

"I'm so happy," he said. "So miserably happy."

The woman laughed, a low, warm sort of laugh. "I'm just plain happy. Do you realize this is our first real breakfast together? A real, proper breakfast in a restaurant?"

I missed whatever the man's answer was because of how hot I suddenly was, my face burning. Did I know the man's voice? Oh, yeah, for absolute sure. It was the voice of Ashanti's dad. As for the woman, her voice was entirely new to me and was absolutely not the voice of Ashanti's mom—as if their conversation would have even made sense in that case. I actually felt dizzy, first time in my life that had happened while I was sitting down. I took a deep breath, and as I did, the woman's booted foot moved, and started feeling around like . . . like she wanted to play footsie or something, which made me want to puke. Her toe bumped the metal center column that held up the table top, and maybe she decided that was his knee, because she gently lowered her foot. But it wasn't his knee, and therefore what she lowered her foot on was the heavy round base of the column, which happened to be where the discarded french fry lay. She stepped right on it, squishing the french fry flat, and sending a tiny spray of ketchup right onto my face.

"Ew," she said.

"What?" said the man—not the man, but Ashanti's father. "Is something wrong?"

"I just stepped on something icky."

Icky? A grown woman just said icky? But no time to reflect on that, because all of a sudden, she was shifting around in her seat and—was it possible? Yes! She was about to peer down under the table to see the exact nature of the ickiness she'd stepped on.

I shrank against the wall, getting as deep as I could into the shadows. The woman's face appeared; the face of the woman I'd seen Ashanti's dad kissing on the street. She was pretty—but nothing like the amazing beauty Ashanti's mom had been and still sort of was—and much younger than I'd thought, maybe under thirty, although the ages of adults were hard to guess. But the main point: she was a lot younger than Ashanti's father.

She peered under the table, shifted her foot to see under it. "French fry," she said, her head then starting to turn in my direction—but at the same time rising up, out of sight. I resumed breathing, and was about to move back to a more comfortable position when Ashanti's father gently put his foot down on hers.

He sighed. "This is so nice," he said. "I just wish—"

"Let's not talk about the future," the woman said. "We should enjoy the time we've got right now."

There was a pause. Then Ashanti's dad said, "I love you," his voice thickening up.

"I love you, too," she said.

My face heated up again, even hotter than before. I didn't want to hear another word, just wanted to be out of there and right away. But how? *Charm! Get me out of here!* No reaction from the charm. The waitress returned and said, "Menus?"

"Please," said Ashanti's dad and his . . . girlfriend? Was that the right word? "Anything you'd recommend?"

How polite he was being, especially compared to Gunn and Kolnikov. I hated him anyway.

But his approach softened up the waitress. "The Provençal omelet is great," she said. "The chef sprinkles on a truffle infusion."

"Sounds perfect," Ashanti's dad said.

"Same for me," said the girlfriend. "Plus a two percent double-shot vanilla latte."

Something about that made Ashanti's dad laugh.

"Stop," the girlfriend said. "Just stop."

The waitress went away.

"You're funny, that's all," said Ashanti's dad.

"Funny good or bad?"

"Good. The best."

They were quiet until the food came. From what I could see of their body positions, I got the idea they were holding hands across the table. I supposed that this was one of the those comfortable silences you hear about; but horribly uncomfortable for me, physically—all scrunched up under the table—and mentally.

They ate. They talked about truffles. Ashanti's dad mentioned an idea for a car commercial he was editing. The girlfriend told him it was brilliant. He told her the inspiration was something she'd said the other night.

"Oh, go on," she said.

He laughed. She joined in. Then he sighed. "I just wish—"

"No," she said, maybe placing her finger across his lips. "No thinking about the future. No worries."

No thinking about the future? No worries? Was she nuts?

Days went by. Maybe weeks. Finally they paid the bill, he took his foot off hers, and they left. I counted silently to sixty and inched out to where I had a view of the surrounding booths. Coast clear. I scrambled up and hurried toward the door. Behind me, I heard the door to the kitchen opening. The waitress called out, "Hey!"

I didn't look back, just ran out of Happy's Place and kept going.

20

No sign of Sheldon Gunn or Kolnikov outside. What did they know about us, the Outlaws? I'd been about to find out when things took a horrible turn; maybe more accurate to say when already horrible things took a horrible turn. But one thing I knew for sure: there was nothing accidental about the death of Mr. Wilders. Did I have any facts? Maybe not actual provable facts. What I had was maybe even more than that, although vaguer at the same time: *And now I come to troublesome professor, handled in the Moscow way.* I didn't have a doubt in my mind. What I had was fear. Were they planning to handle us in the Moscow way too?

I got lost in all these dark thoughts, and the next thing I knew, I was back home in our building, trudging up the stairs to our apartment. I unlocked the door and went inside. Mom was at the laptop in the kitchen, typing real fast.

"Hi, Mom," I said, and suddenly was right on the point of letting tons of stuff come spilling out.

"Hi, Robbie," she said, not looking up. "Still raining outside?"

All she had to do was glance out the window. But actually I didn't know either—that was how out of it I'd been—so I had to glance out the window myself.

"More like snow now," I told her.

"Uh-huh," she said.

Tap tap, tap tap—her fingers were practically a blur. Maybe it was bad of me, but I wanted them to stop.

"What are you writing?" I said.

Her fingers, nails bitten right down—when had that happened?—went still, hovering over the keyboard. My mom looked up. "A sort of proposal," she said. "I'm applying for an in-house job."

I'd heard of in-house jobs: a way for lawyers to still make good money without having to be the fastest rat in the race.

"What does it pay?" I said, the question just blurting itself out.

My mom's eyebrows rose. "Cutting to the chase, huh?" she said.

"Sorry," I said. "But will we be able to buy the building? Mitch is thinking of selling."

"Probably not enough," my mom said. "And how did

you know? Did you see the real estate agent on your way up?"

"Real estate agent?"

"I think they've got a potential buyer downstairs at this very moment."

"Already?"

She rested her hands on the table. "But it's nothing for us to worry about," my mom said. "Tenants have lots of rights in this city, and if at some point we have to move, there'd be plenty of time to find a place we liked."

"Okay. Thanks, Mom."

Her fingers hooked themselves in a purposeful way and returned to the keyboard. I went upstairs with no plan, and stood in my room kind of paralyzed, staring out the window. This wasn't the kind of paralysis where you didn't know what to do. This was the kind where you knew but couldn't face doing it. I had to tell Ashanti what I'd seen and heard. And it had to be in person. In person was the hardest of all the possible communication methods, but I just sort of knew that if you were communicating something hard, then the method had to be hard, too.

At least, as I gazed out my window, I knew it for a little while. Then I began to backtrack, thinking, for example, what if things were reversed and I was in Ashanti's place? Wouldn't I want to know? At first, I was sure I would, but then I started asking myself why. Knowing would be a terrible burden, the unbundling of which would lead to awful scenes and almost certainly the breakup of the family. So maybe some things were better not to know. But I already knew! Why did that have to happen? Didn't we have enough going on? I started feeling a little sorry for myself. Feeling sorry for yourself can actually feel kind of good, in a way, sort of like a low-grade fever, just enough to stay home from school and lie in bed, the mind having weirder than usual thoughts but not too weird.

I heard voices down below. There's a garden behind the building, a small space with a brick patio and a dirt patch where Mitch had tried planting tomatoes, eggplant, and quinoa, all unsuccessfully. I looked down and saw a real estate agent, tablet and clipboard in hand, talking to someone out of sight, most likely standing just inside Mitch's sliding door to the garden. You see lots of real estate agents in Brooklyn. Most are women, always well-dressed and well-groomed, often wearing makeup that softened faces that could use a little softening. I put my ear close to the glass.

". . . and eighty square feet," the real estate agent was saying. "Up above," she went on, tilting back her head and starting to point my way—I quickly withdrew a step or so—"we have those two fire-escape-type balconies, which I'm sure could be expanded, although you'd have to go through a permitting process."

A man spoke. "I like it," he said.

"You like the balcony idea?" said the real estate agent.

I moved back to the window, couldn't help myself. There was something so familiar about the man's voice. "I like house," he said, still out of sight. "Will buy."

"Uh," said the agent, her lips turning up in smile formation, "you want to submit an offer?"

"Full price," the man said.

"Good idea," the agent said. "It really is a gem. Why don't we go out to the car, and I'll write up the—"

"Full offer plus ten percent," the man said.

The agent blinked.

"Ten percent extra for present owner leaving at once."

"At once?"

"Twenty percent is possible."

More blinking. "I'm sorry?"

"Perhaps for negotiation point," the man said. "Keep under hat. Agreed?"

"Um, yes, yes, of course," said the agent. "Agreed. So we write up an offer for the full price plus ten percent, contingent on immediate occupancy?"

"Is correct. Cash offer."

"Very good. Let's go to the car and write up—"

"You write. I sign now."

"Certainly." The agent flipped through pages on her clipboard. "Just sign here."

The man stepped into view, pen in hand. A blond man; his shoulders and chest seemed even more immense from this up-above angle. It was Kolnikov. I got lightheaded from the merest sight of him, actually started swaying, my legs were so weak. When I looked again half a minute or so later—having gotten a grip, even wished for a flowerpot—they were both gone.

Immediate occupancy? What did that mean? The Moscow way. Kolnikov was coming after me, about to invade my home. He could own my apartment today. He could be moving in, actually living right down below us, maybe moving around in the night while me and my family slept right above. Movements I might even hear, due to this strange quirky thing about my closet—a trick of the pipes, my dad said—when sometimes I could hear Mitch quite clearly. I opened my closet door, and yes, it was happening right now.

Mitch's voice rose from below, sounding not like he was two floors down in his own place, but in the next room. "Ten percent over asking? What's that all about?"

"An incentive to move things along," the agent said. "A little quicker than normal."

"How much quicker?"

"Like yesterday."

"Yesterday?"

"I exaggerate, but only a little."

"Give me twenty minutes to think it over," Mitch said.

"I'll be in my car," said the agent. "It's a fabulous offer, as I'm sure you realize, so please try to be quick—the client's waiting for my call."

I knocked on Mitch's door. From inside, he called, "Hey! It's nowhere near twenty minutes yet." I knocked harder. The door opened, and Mitch looked out, pen and paper in hand. "Oh, it's you," he said. "Uh, Robbie. I was expecting someone else."

"Like who?" I said. Uh-oh. Where had that come from?

"Huh? What business is it of yours?" Mitch said. "I can't believe I heard that."

Off to a bad start. I wanted to run. But why be afraid of Mitch—unshaven, breath not too good, pimple on the side of his nose? I spoke to the pimple.

"Don't sign that offer," I said.

Mitch rocked back. "Offer? How do you know about any offer?"

Good question. The truth was not going to help. Something juicier was needed, and fast. "I can't tell you—it's too dangerous."

"Huh?"

"The point is—sign that offer, and you'll end up in jail."

"Jail?"

"Federal prison. Or state. Or possibly both. The buyer is a criminal—an international criminal with plans to lure you into a dangerous conspiracy."

Mitch's eyebrows—thick and kind of wild—rose into two sharp and hairy upside-down Vs. "How do you know?"

"I already told you—it's too dangerous." His eyes narrowed. Was he buying it? Maybe not. "I have connections. Let's leave it like that."

"Connections? From Thatcher? Is that what you're saying?"

"All I can tell you is that it's the kind of place where the DA sends her kid." Which happened to be true, although the DA's kid was a junior who probably didn't even know I existed.

Mitch thought for a moment, then sighed. "The way of the world—it's always the same."

Which I didn't exactly get; all I knew was that my approach was working like . . . like a charm. "Do yourself a favor and rip up that offer."

Mitch gazed down unhappily at the paper. "I sure could use that money."

"Can't spend it in lockup. And the Feds will take it all anyway."

"In penalties?"

"The harshest."

"Then there's no choice."

"None."

Mitch tore the paper to shreds. I picked up the scraps and handed them to him. "Go give this to the agent and tell her she's all done."

"Are you saying she's in on the conspiracy, too?"

"You never know. That's the whole point of conspiracies."

Yes, like a charm. But from the actual charm, nothing. As Mitch headed outside to the agent's car, I felt it hanging cold and unhelpful around my neck.

21

My mom was still on her laptop when I let myself back into our apartment.

"Where were you?" she said. "I didn't even hear you leave."

"Just stepped out for . . . for a breath of air."

My mom gave me a look. Why was it so hard to put things past her?

"On account of it's so nasty out there," I added quickly, an addition that made zero sense, absolutely pitiful.

Her face changed, got a lot warmer. "You're bored, aren't you?"

"Oh, no, Mom, not at all."

"Of course you are. Not much of a vacation for you, is it? But—fingers crossed—next year will be better. I promise. Did you know Chas wrote ten pages yesterday?"

"About the one-armed detective?"

My mom nodded. "The most he's ever done in a day,

by far. And even better, he e-mailed the pages to George Gentry, and Gentry loved them."

"Wow. That's great. What did Dad say?"

"To Gentry? He was actually sort of gruff, I thought."

"Uh-oh."

"It won't matter. Writers are allowed to be difficult."

"Then that's what I'll be when I grow up."

"Seriously?"

"No."

My mom laughed, then got back to work. I went upstairs, heard my dad tapping at his keyboard, peeked into the office.

"Hey, Dad, congrats. I hear the guy loved what you did."

My dad turned to me. Normally when he worked he looked terrible, all tense and exhausted, but now he seemed fresh and rested. "Thanks," he said. "It looks like I've got the instinct for writing the exact right level of crap."

"Um, uh."

"Can't teach that, Robbie. You have it or you don't."

So it was a joke? He was happy doing this job? Yes? No? I took a chance and laughed. My dad looked like he was about to laugh, too, and although he didn't, I still left with the impression that he was doing all right. As I went back to my own room—Pendleton still asleep on the bed—it hit me that I liked my parents. I loved them—went without saying—but now I realized I also liked them. Kind of a whacked-out thought, and then came another: there was more free choice in liking than loving. One more thing about my parents, a weird thought for their own kid to be having, but they were kind of innocent in some ways. That made me all the more relieved that I'd foiled Kolnikov, at least for now, and he wouldn't be threatening us from inside the building.

At least for now.

Pendleton opened his eyes, seemed to take in my presence, yawned, and returned to dreamland.

At least for now. I couldn't get rid of those four words. We had enemies, and our enemies had plans. What were those plans? Detonation was part of it. What had Kolnikov said? *Deep down under. Speciality of my company, in fact, but all inclusive in price.* And there was more, what Kolnikov had called *potentiality issue number two—the snooping wretches: these kids.*

Those were the facts, huge and looming. I gazed at my phone, working up the nerve to call Ashanti and arrange a face-to-face, get that part over with. My nerve resisted being worked up, and my mind got busy with all sorts of avoidance schemes, in which I was tangled when the phone rang: Ashanti.

Like a—yes, wretch, a wretched coward—I hesitated

for five whole rings before my better nature stepped up to the plate.

"Hi, Ashanti," I said.

"Let me guess," she said. "You were in the shower."

"Um, ah," I said. "Pendleton."

"That was my second guess."

I laughed. Ashanti joined in. Was just after laughing the time for dropping the bomb? Before I could even start wrestling with that one, Ashanti had gone on.

"Things are better now," she said.

"Huh? What things?"

"With my mom. The doctor came. He thinks she was dehydrated."

"Oh."

"So my dad filled the fridge with all these hydrating drinks from Finland."

"Finland?"

"He found out they're the best."

"Oh."

"But that's not why I called."

"No?"

"What's with you?" Ashanti said. "You've gone all one-wordy on me, girl."

"Me?"

"Ha-ha. You're not funny."

"I'm just, um, distracted right now."

"By what?"

"All these developments."

"Like what?"

Development one was her own cheating dad. I skipped that one—had to be done in person, right?—and went right to Tut-Tut and how they'd moved him to a new lockup and then to getting chased by Kolnikov and Henkel, which took me to what I'd heard at Happy's Place.

Ashanti cut in. "Kolnikov was talking about us?"

"But I didn't catch that part," I said. "This other—these people came and sat down right at the table I was under."

"Oh, my God."

"Yeah."

"What did you do?"

"Just sort of scrunched up."

"How many of them were there?"

"Two."

One more question—just one—and it was all going to come spilling out.

"You know what I think we should do?" Ashanti said.

Okay. Maybe not that question.

"What?"

"Talk to Dina DeNunzio."

"About what?"

"Everything," Ashanti said.

"Everything?"

"Well, maybe not everything, if you're talking about you know what, but she clearly has doubts about how they're saying Mr. Wilders died, and now we know this whole Moscow way thing."

Dina, like Kolnikov, had made an attempt to invade my home. Maybe not as menacing, but actually more successful. "Can we trust her?" I said.

"Probably not. But have you got a better idea?"

"Nope."

"Just hanging with Ashanti for a while," I called over my shoulder as I headed downstairs. Through Mitch's door in the hall came saxophone sounds, some morose tune, which I took to mean that Mitch was back to spinning his wheels.

Outside the snow had turned back to rain and the wind was rising. Ashanti was already on the sidewalk, walking toward me under a big black umbrella.

"Quick," she said. "Get under."

So there we were, close together in a small dry space, person to person, the proper setup for delivering bad news. I shot her a quick sideways glance. She looked happy, her skin glowing, energy just radiating off her. Why? Because her mom was doing better? Because we were about to get help from Dina DeNunzio, an adult with real power? I didn't know, and it didn't matter. I was about to shatter her mood, real fast and maybe for a long time to come.

"Ashanti?" I said.

"Yeah?"

"Um."

And just as I was about to plunge ahead with no real plan and my heart beating faster and faster, a voice called out, "Hey! You guys!"

We turned and saw Silas hurrying toward us across the street. He wore a bright orange poncho over his Michelin-Man jacket, which made him seem very wide, and also had on a fisherman's rain hat that was way too big for him, the ear flaps sticking out straight sideways for some reason, rain running off them and onto his shoulders. He stepped right into the gutter, making an enormous splash, but on account of knee-length green rubber boots, didn't get his feet wet.

"Hey! You guys!" He ran up to us, shedding water like a storm all his own. "Wait up."

"Hi," Ashanti said, her voice as gentle as I'd ever heard it. "What's up?"

Silas stood before us, huffing and puffing. When he'd caught his breath, he said, "Hi." He opened his mouth, seemed about to say more, but did not.

"Hi," Ashanti said again.

"Hi," I said. "Something on your mind?"

Silas nodded.

"Like what?" I said.

He shrugged. Silas at a loss for words? That wasn't him at all.

"You want us to guess?" I said.

He smiled a tiny smile, there and gone. "Yeah, maybe I do. The thing is . . ." He looked down, shuffled his feet. "It turns out, um, I had a father after all. What if he'd lived? You never know."

Meaning he and Silas might have ended up with a good relationship? "Yeah," I said.

Ashanti laid a hand on Silas's shoulder. "Which is a pretty good reason for us to find out what happened to him."

"And make them sorry," I said.

"Them?" Silas said.

I told him about the Moscow way. A strange thing happened to his face while I was explaining. It seemed to get thinner and older, like we were getting a glimpse of how he'd look grown up—actually kind of strong and handsome.

"We need a plan," he said.

We sat at a back table at Monsieur Señor's, the coffee place where my dad and other writers went when they cracked under the pressure of piling up the words all on their lonesomes.

"Monsieur Señor's?" said Silas, removing layer after layer of clothing and dampening everything in sight. "That's humor, right?" he went on, starting to sound more like himself. "I like it. You could also do it the other way—Señor Monsieur's—but all in all I think—"

He stopped talking and sniffed the air. I noticed for the first time how sort of mobile Silas's nose was and guessed he had an off-the-charts sense of smell. "Let's get our order in," he said.

Hugh, the barista, who was in the middle of having all his tattoos removed—the snake wrapped around his neck couldn't disappear fast enough for me—arrived with three steaming mugs of hot chocolate. "Enjoy."

Silas tasted his hot chocolate. "Wow. This is the best I've ever tasted." Hugh laughed and went away. Silas lowered his voice. "Was that a hipster kind of laugh?"

"Huh?" I said.

"He's a hipster, right?" Silas said. "Isn't this a hipster kind of place?"

Which was one of those Silas-type tangents that often made Ashanti impatient, but now she smiled a teasing sort of smile and said, "Figuring on being a hipster when you grow up?"

Silas shook his head. "When I grow up, I want to be an engineer for an asteroid mining company."

I just gazed at him. Silas was amazing in his own way.

Then I got even more amazed when Ashanti said, "Good idea."

"Hey, thanks," said Silas.

"No problem," Ashanti said. Then she rapped her knuckles on the table. "To business."

"Ashanti wants to bring in Dina DeNunzio," I said. "And I think it's a good idea."

"Are you going to tell her about the"—he lowered his voice to a sort of stage whisper that actually carried very well, so well that Hugh, over by the coffee machines, turned his head our way—"you know what?"

"Not unless we have to," said Ashanti.

"She won't believe it," Silas said. "And she'll think we're nuts."

"Maybe it'll do something to convince her," I said. I glanced around. Hugh had gone back to foaming and frothing, and no one else was interested in us. I took off the charm and laid it on the table. We stared at it.

"Do something," Silas commanded.

But the charm just sat there, looking like a small metal heart, kind of cheap and not even well-shaped for a heart, being too wide at the bottom and rounded instead of pointed. I put my finger on one edge. The others did the same, so we were all in contact with the charm. It did nothing, refusing to heat up or cooperate in the slightest way.

"Let's vote," I said. "All in favor of calling Dina?"

Ashanti took her finger off the charm and raised her hand. So did I. Silas alone was still touching the charm.

"Does it have to be unanimous?" he said.

"What do you think?" said Ashanti.

"What do I think?" Silas answered. "I'm not so sure about democracy, for starters. There's a lot to be said for dictatorship, the benevolent kind, to say nothing of—"

"Silas!" Ashanti and I said together.

"She'll think we're nuts," he repeated. "And there are lots of other risks as well." He glanced around. "Do you want me to go into them?" Silence. "I suppose not. But I will anyway. For example, all of a sudden we're cool with trusting adults?"

Ashanti stared hard at the wall, almost like she was trying to see right through it. "I go back and forth on that," she said.

Uh-oh. The Ashanti problem was with me all the time, even when I'd succeeded in burying it.

"It's not so much about trusting adults," I said, "as this particular adult. She's no friend of Sheldon Gunn."

I turned to Silas, waited for him to demolish my argument. Silas surprised me. Slowly and reluctantly, like it weighed a thousand pounds, he raised his hand.

"All opposed?" I said, not to be funny, but because of a sudden hunch that the charm might want a say at this point. But it remained inert. "Three yesses, no noes."

"What about Tut-Tut?" Silas said.

"We'll have to vote for him," I replied. "For now."

"Can't you just see him raising his hand?" said Ashanti.

I could, and easily. "That makes four," I said. "We call Dina. Who wants to do it?"

No one wanted to do it.

"I nominate you," Silas said.

"Second," said Ashanti.

The vote was two to one in favor of me making the call, with only me opposed. I called Dina at the TV station. They transferred the call, and she answered while the first ring was still ringing.

"DeNunzio," she said, quick, crisp, strictly business. Being a reporter would be cool for sure; I put that thought aside for later.

"Um, hi," I said. "It's Robbie. Robbie Forester." There was a pause, and for a moment, I wondered if I'd gotten everything wrong. "We met a couple of—"

"I know who you are," Dina said. "What's up?"

"We, uh, want to talk to you."

"What about?"

"Mr. Wilders."

Another pause. I was sure I could feel her thinking, real fast. "Where are you?" she said.

"In Brooklyn," I replied, real nonspecific, as though her quick-thinking ability had somehow spread to me.

"At home?"

"No," I said. "We could come to you."

"The station's in Manhattan," she said. "Tell you what—I'll come to you. Name a place."

Name a place? Not this place: much too public. I covered the phone with my hand and whispered, "She wants to meet somewhere."

"Not here," said Ashanti and Silas together.

"Joe Louis?" I said. They nodded. I uncovered the mouthpiece. "Do you know Joe Louis School?"

"See you there in forty-five minutes," Dina said.

Hugh brought the bill. Then came a big surprise. Silas reached into his pocket, pulled out four twenties, two fives, and a one.

"You made that on your printer?" Ashanti said.

"I suppose I could have," Silas said, "but the fact is I earned it doing honest work."

"Like what?"

"I got Mrs. Rubinstein's computer up and running for her—she's the neighbor down the hall. She was so grateful she paid me a hundred bucks."

"How long did it take?" I said, wondering if Silas could turn this into a real career.

"A couple of seconds," he said. "It wasn't plugged in."

"Which you told her in this honest working way of yours?"

"Actually not," Silas said. "What if she felt

embarrassed, like she was dumb or something? So I fooled around with it for a while, upgraded a few things, and downloaded a cool game about these giant ants biting the heads off of anybody you choose."

"Mrs. Rubinstein wants to play a game like that?" I said.

"Can't say for sure. She doesn't know she has it."

22

Joe Louis was a shabby old brick building on a shabby street that was just around the corner from a fancy one, a common situation in Brooklyn. It had a small, paved schoolyard with a single backboard, although as we walked up, I saw that the hoop, which had always lacked a net, was now itself missing. We crossed the yard and stood under the overhang at the school entrance, out of the rain.

Silas checked the time. "Eighteen more minutes," he said.

"What if she brings a camera crew?" Ashanti said.

I hadn't thought of that, had no answer. No one had an answer. We stood in silence, eventually slumping down into sitting positions, our backs to the door. The wind blew scraps of this and that across the pavement. No talking happened. I felt kind of alone, which didn't make sense: these were my best friends! But a horrible feeling was growing like a dark thing inside me, a feeling that all this friendship was now at risk of getting trampled or thrown away.

"Two minutes," Silas said.

We rose, looked west, where Dina would be coming from if she'd taken the subway. Then we looked east, where she'd appear if she was driving, Joe Louis being on a one-way street. It was one of those weird big-city moments when no people or cars were around and you could almost imagine yourself the only living inhabitant.

"Time," said Silas.

A car drove by, and then another, followed by a steady stream, windshield wipers whipping back and forth. And now there were pedestrians, most alone, all of them hurrying to get out of the rain. But no sign of Dina.

"It's been an hour," Silas said. "I'm freezing."

"Why don't you give her a call?" Ashanti said.

"Okay." I redialed the station, again was put through to Dina, but this time she didn't pick up and I got sent to voice mail.

"Hi, it's Robbie. We're at Joe Louis. Are you—I mean—um, should we keep waiting? Or . . ." I clicked off.

"Smooth," said Silas.

My voice rose. "Zip it!" All at once I was real angry, not knowing why. I paced around a bit, even kicked at the brick wall. I found myself wishing Tut-Tut was here.

Ashanti came over and gave me a light pat on the shoulder. I calmed down.

We waited for another half hour and then left, heading toward the subway station on our way back to HQ, although I wasn't sure why: I was out of ideas. Just before the subway entrance stood a newspaper stand with a cold-looking turbaned guy inside. His attention was on a small TV propped up on some magazines. On the screen—for just a second before a toothpaste commercial—was a still picture of Dina DeNunzio, with a caption that read MISSING.

"Missing?" I said.

The newsstand guy turned to us. "Terrible, terrible news," he said, speaking in an Indian accent—the kind from India—that makes English suddenly sound so musical. "I myself am the biggest possible fan of Dina DeNunzio."

"But what happened to her?" Ashanti said. "What did they say on TV?"

He shrugged. "A paucity of facts—that is the problem. It seems Miss DeNunzio left the office and was last seen driving away in her car. The car was found thirty minutes ago—door open and engine running, very bad—and no sign of her."

"Found where?" Silas said.

The newsstand guy paused before answering, giving us a careful scan. "You, too, are fans of Dina?"

We all nodded.

"I think they were referencing somewhere in Dumbo," the newsstand guy said. "Down under the bridges."

Dumbo is one of the very coolest parts of Brooklyn, at least for now; these things can change pretty fast. It borders on the river, right where the Manhattan and Brooklyn Bridges come close to each other. We took a cab, on account of Silas's recent windfall. He sat up front with the driver—which is where you never want to sit in a cab—and Ashanti and I sat in back. Silas didn't seem at all uncomfortable up there, was soon involved in a conversation, and not long after that, he was busy upgrading all the driver's electronic devices—phone, tablet, GPS.

We arrived in Dumbo, bumped along on a cobblestone road. "Anywhere special?" said the driver.

"The sculpture park," Silas told him.

I leaned forward. "Why there?"

"Trust me," Silas said, sounding even smugger than usual, not bothering to turn his head. I guessed that he'd picked up some info on the driver's tablet; maybe I was starting to know how his mind worked.

The driver turned a corner, drove under the shadow of one of the bridges, reached the river, and came to a stop. "Can't go any more," he said, pointing ahead. "Police activity."

Up ahead I saw the sculpture park, a small green space bordering the river, now blocked off by squad cars, their blue lights flashing wetly in the rain. Tall insect-like sculptures towered over everything, all of them the color of dark clouds. We got out.

"No charge," the cabbie said. Had that ever happened before in the whole history of New York?

And as we walked away, Ashanti—not for the first time—spoke my thought aloud. "Has that ever happened before in the whole history of New York?"

"Sure," Silas said. "All the time with movie stars and athletes."

We approached the police line. Crime scene tape was still going up. Beyond it I could see some cops gathered around a car parked on the grass, maybe twenty feet from the road. The driver's side door hung open, as the newsstand guy had said, but the engine was no longer running. A plainclothes cop with POLICE on the back of his blue jacket leaned into the car, taking pictures. Without a word between us, we all moved beyond the farthest reach of the crime scene tape, stepped up on the grass and walked toward the car.

Everyone was so busy that we went unnoticed. I didn't know what was drawing Ashanti and Silas, but as for me, I was hoping not to see things—terrible things like blood, for example, or clumps of hair, or bullet holes in a cool red leather jacket. I saw none of that, nothing bad at all, just a car sitting where it shouldn't have been; and no driver.

Then came a booming voice, real angry. "Hey, you kids! What do you think you're doing?"

I whipped around.

A huge cop was coming toward us, waving his arms. "Can't you stupid kids even read?"

We started to move away.

"Hold it right there!"

I paused, so close to taking off. But running away from cops didn't seem like a plan, certainly not when one of the runners was Silas. The cop came right up to us, towering enormously, his face all red, rain dripping off the bill of his hat.

"We, uh, were just looking," I began, "and—"

"Saw it on the news, officer," Silas broke in. "Any sign of Dina DeNunzio? We're big fans. What happened here?"

I'd heard of faces turning purple before but never actually seen it. Now I did for the first time. "Shut up!" the cop yelled. "Let's see some ID."

"We don't have any ID," Ashanti said.

"We're kids," I added, one of the feeblest remarks of my whole life.

"Don't feed me that," the cop said, adding another word I won't repeat. "You're all school age, meaning you've got student ID." He held out his hand.

The truth was I didn't have my student ID on me; no reason to, with my MetroCard pass. And what if he wrote down our names, contacted our parents, or even Thatcher? "Um, it's vacation," I said.

The cop turned his full attention on me. "Oh, a smart-ass, huh? Maybe somebody should teach you some—"

He paused. Silas had reached into his pocket, was taking out what looked like some kind of plastic ID cards.

"I happen to be carrying the IDs, officer," he said, handing them to the cop.

The cop peered at the first one, then eyed Silas. "Brock McCool?" he said.

"That's me," said Silas.

The cop nodded, checked the next ID, turned to Ashanti. "Tiffany Strong?"

"Uh," said Ashanti. "Um, yeah."

And then it was my turn. "Maxine Rumble?"

"Call me Max," I told the cop.

He handed the cards back to Silas. "Okay—now get lost!"

We backed away on a sort of tide of relief. As soon as we were out of the cop's hearing distance, Ashanti and I rounded on Silas.

"Whoa," he said. "I thought we might need fake IDs one day, so I made some. And I was right! So what's the problem?"

"Tiffany?" said Ashanti.

"Maxine?" I said.

"Yes," Silas said. "What am I missing?"

I didn't know where to begin. And even if I had, there was no time. Where was Dina? She'd been on her way to meet us. What had happened to her? This—I took one last quick glance—didn't look like a car accident: her car was undamaged. The whole situation looked more like—

Whoa! What was that I saw low down on the driver's-side rear door of the Dina's car? I took a few sideways steps, got a better angle. A muddy footprint, half washed away by the rain, but the kind of footprint left by a boot with deep treads, was just visible on the lower part of the rear door. How would a footprint get left in a place like that? What if some guy was bracing himself against the car while he tried to force open the front door, a front door that was stuck for some reason? One more thing: the mud was a strange sort of mud, very darkish. A mud I knew. A sickening idea began forming in my mind, an idea that seemed to come sneaking back from the near future.

We walked away from the sculpture park, crossed the street, and stood under the awning of a wine shop. Through the foggy window I saw a few people swirling glasses, sniffing at them, wrinkling up their foreheads in deep thought. What a world—on the far side of that window, just a few feet away, there was nothing to worry about except the taste of wine.

"Kolnikov's got her," I said. I explained about the boot mark and the mud.

"Where?" Ashanti said.

"Could be anywhere," said Silas.

"I'm not so sure about that," I said; my mind was on one word: *detonation.*

Inside the wine shop, a fat guy in one of those Irish fisherman sweaters spat a thin red stream into a bowl.

"What's with the whole wine thing?" Silas said.

"Never mind that," I told him. "We have to think."

"All right. Here's a thought. Let's call the cops."

"No way," Ashanti said.

"Why not?" said Silas.

"First, we don't know anything about Kolnikov, even if that's his real name. Second, they'll never believe us about Sheldon Gunn. Third, he'll find out and then . . ."

Ashanti was right. I didn't even want to let number three play out in my mind.

"Then we need a plan," Silas said.

"You keep saying that—it's not helpful." I glanced around. It was getting dark: night had snuck up on us, the way it sometimes did in the city. "Supposing," I began, and then my cell phone rang. I checked the screen: *Silas*. I showed it to him. "Someone's calling me on your phone."

"My phone?" He patted his pockets. Silas had a lot of pockets, so it took some time. "Where is it?"

"Maybe if I answer, we'll find out." I pressed the green button. "Hello?"

A voice spoke, a voice that wavered somewhere between kid and man. "Hey. Silas there?"

"Thaddeus?" Silas said, hovering in close. He snatched the phone from me. "You stole my phone?"

Before Silas clamped the phone to his ear, I could just make out Thaddeus's voice on the other end. He sounded like Silas, except older and not as nice.

"More like borrowing it," he said.

Silas had a roundish kind of face on which you hardly ever saw anger, but it was visible now. "Why? Where's Mom? I want to—"

He went silent, seemed to be listening very hard. His eyes opened wide. "Oh, my God," he said. "All right—we're coming." He pocketed the phone in a dazed sort of way.

"We're coming?" Ashanti said. "Where?"

"My place," Silas said. "Dina's hiding out there. She wants us."

23

What's she doing there?" I said.

Silas shrugged.

"She must have escaped," Ashanti said.

"But how would she even know where I live?" Silas asked.

"She knows where I live," I said. "She's a reporter—she finds things out."

"Especially about us," Ashanti added.

"Yeah," I said. "But we're sort of on the same side with her. And now she needs our help."

They nodded. Silas lived a couple of miles away in a not-very-high high-rise near the beginning of the Gowanus Canal. "Thaddeus says she wants us to take a taxi," Silas said. "She'll pay us back."

"That won't be necessary," Ashanti said. "Not with you being loaded at present."

Silas looked to be formulating some comeback, but at

that moment, a taxi went by. Silas raised his hand. The taxi pulled right over, the quickest response I'd ever seen from a New York cab. We jumped in.

Silas, in front—"I like to see where I'm going," he said—gave his address. The driver nodded and hit the button on the meter. From where I sat in the backseat behind the driver, I couldn't see much of him, just a thick neck and a thick bald head, plus big fleshy ears. He turned a corner, bumped across a cobblestone street down under one of the bridges, then sped up a hill, cutting off another car that gave an angry honk. All New York cabbies drove the same way, like being over-the-top aggressive was one of the requirements.

"Hey," said Silas, a few blocks later, "shouldn't you have turned back there?"

"Is faster like this," the driver said. He had a low, growly voice, and also an accent, which was pretty much another characteristic of New York cabbies.

The driver made a few more darting moves that resulted in lots of honking, then turned left, right, and left again in quick succession, and suddenly we were crossing Flatbush Avenue. Whoa. That couldn't be a faster way to Silas's building, in fact was totally wrong. I glanced at Silas. He was gazing out the side window; I imagined his face—how it gets when he's lost in some completely irrelevant thought.

"Silas?" I said.

"What?" He glanced around. "Hey," he said again, "was that Flatbush?"

"Yes," I said, raising my voice. "He's way off course."

The driver shrugged. "Is faster."

Ashanti leaned into the opening in the Plexiglas partition. "It isn't faster. Turn around. We're in a hurry."

"Sure, sure," said the driver. "Keep on hat." But he showed not the slightest sign of turning around. Instead he zipped into a narrow alley lined with grimy buildings and said "keep on hat" a few more times. And all at once, maybe a little late, I caught on to that accent: Russian, no doubt about it.

I banged on the partition. "Stop the car! Stop right this second!"

The driver didn't stop. Instead he sped up even more, fishtailing a bit and knocking over a whole row of trash cans. We were going way too fast to consider jumping out, but just as I began considering it all the same, the door locks snapped down. I tried to snap mine back up, couldn't budge it. The driver reached around and closed the sliding partition window with a hard bang.

"Silas! Grab the keys!"

"The keys?" he said, starting to turn in my direction. The driver must have thought Silas was going to do exactly what I'd told him and pronto—which wasn't Silas at all. With Silas now would come lots of back-andforthing about the odds of successfully grabbing the keys, or whether it would even stop the car in the first place, or other possibilities I hadn't imagined. But the driver didn't know Silas. Or maybe he was simply a mean and violent person—because with no warning and real quick, he jabbed his right elbow at Silas's face. *Jab* is maybe the wrong word if you don't think jabs can be hard. The driver's jab was very hard. It made him grunt with effort as he delivered the blow, a blow that caught Silas square on the jaw as he was turning toward me. There was a loud thud; Silas's eyeballs rolled up, exposing the whites of his eyes, and he slumped motionless against the door.

I clawed at the partition window: locked in place, immovable. Ashanti went crazy. She rocked back on the seat, raised her legs and started kicking at the Plexiglas with amazing strength, rocking the whole cab. But she got nowhere with the Plexiglas, which, I remembered, was bulletproof. Still, it was good to see the driver glance back with real fear on his face, one of those faces where all the lines slanted down.

The driver whipped around, hunched over the wheel, and stepped on it even more. Up ahead, the alley was coming to a T-type intersection with another alley. At this speed, there was no way we'd ever be able to make the turn. Were we going to crash into those buildings at the end, splintering into one of the garage doors facing this second alley? I held on to Ashanti. She held on to me. The distance narrowed down to practically nothing, and as I tensed for the impact, the garage door directly in our path flew open. The driver hit the brakes, and we went squealing into the garage, up a ramp, and into a big enclosed trailer—although I couldn't be sure about that because of how shadowy things suddenly got. We banged into the far end wall of the trailer, if that was what it was, but not hard, since we'd slowed down a lot by then, and before I knew what was going on, the driver had switched off the engine and jumped out of the cab. I twisted around, and through the rear window saw him running toward a rectangle of late-evening light—yes, we were in a trailer—and then jumping right outside. The double cargo doors at the back of the trailer closed with a solid thump, and we were in total darkness.

We went still. I tried my door. Locked. I fiddled with buttons and things I felt on the inside of the door, got nowhere. I could hear Ashanti doing the same thing.

"Ashanti?"

"Nope. But the controls are in front. Silas—you hear that?"

No answer.

"Silas," I said, "find the controls."

No answer.

"Silas? Silas?"

Silence.

Suddenly Ashanti dug her fingers into my arm, very hard. "I can't breathe!"

"Just take it slow," I said. "There's air."

Her voice rose, way up into a sort of hysteria I'd never heard from her, could hardly believe her capable of. "I can't breathe! I can't breathe!"

Something had to be done, and at the moment, there didn't seem to be anyone to do it but me. Would the side windows be unbreakable, too? I wriggled around, got in position, gathered my strength, and—*Smash!*—I kicked out the window on my side. I scrambled out, feeling my way in the darkness, and opened the driver's door. The ceiling light flashed on, pushing back the darkness.

Ashanti, in the backseat, let out a deep breath. Her face was the color of ashes. I snapped open the master lock on the side of the door, and she got out. I took a quick look around—yes, we were in a taxi inside an otherwise empty trailer—and then turned to Silas. He lay on the front seat, eyes closed. I put my face close to his and felt his breath on my skin.

"Is he breathing?" Ashanti said, opening the door on Silas's side. "Tell me he's breathing."

"He's breathing."

Ashanti leaned in, started rubbing Silas's hands. "Silas, come on, wake up. Please."

Silas showed no sign of waking up, just lay there breathing softly, a dark bruise forming on his jaw. We left him and went to the cargo doors. It looked like they might be opened with a big lever handle thing, but we couldn't move it an inch.

"Locked from the outside," Ashanti said. Her face was less ashy now, but far from normal.

"What are we going to do?" I said, a stupid and weak remark I regretted at once.

Ashanti whipped out her phone. Of course!

"No service," she said. "You?"

I tried my phone. "Nope. What about pounding on the doors?"

We wondered about that—potential risks and rewards—and while I was wondering, I heard Silas: *Doesn't seem like a clever idea to me. Just sayin'. As for the cell phones, it's not a no-service issue. They're jamming us.*

"Silas?" I said. We hurried back to the taxi, looked in through the door—left open so we'd have light. "You all right?" Ashanti said.

But Silas was just lying there the way we'd left him, eyes closed, his breathing slow and regular.

"Silas?" I said. I turned to Ashanti. "Didn't you just hear him? I couldn't have imagined it."

"Loud and clear," Ashanti said. "Silas? This no time for your stupid games."

He lay there. He breathed. Then it hit me. I touched the charm: it was heating up.

"Feel," I said.

Ashanti touched the charm. "It's back?"

"Finally," I said.

"Why now?" Ashanti said.

"I don't know. Maybe the Canarsee spirits are getting mad at last."

We gazed at Silas. When the charm was working, it gave him telepathic power, meaning he was still out cold, but we were getting insights from his unconscious mind.

"Come on, Silas," I said.

"We need you," Ashanti said.

That goes without saying.

"Don't be a jerk," Ashanti said. "Wake up."

I'm not sleeping, you morons. That guy knocked me out. Are you blind? I'm out cold. How come you're not getting that? And did you hear his accent? He's in cahoots with Kolnikov, for sure.

"Cahoots?" Ashanti said. "When you're knocked out, your brain is using words like *cahoots*? Wake up this second!"

Silas showed no sign of waking up. If we had some water, maybe we could—

I heard noises from outside. Ashanti and I turned toward the trailer's double doors just in time to see them getting whipped open. By whom was hard to say, on account of it now being black night outside. But whoever it was threw in a long, dark bundle. It landed with a thud. The doors slammed shut. Some kind of bolt thunked into place.

Ashanti and I moved toward the bundle, slow and cautious. It was a rolled-up tarp, not quite still. We knelt and started unrolling the tarp. There was a person inside! The head came into view, a head with cheerleader-style hair, the eyes and mouth both duct-taped over. We carefully stripped off the duct tape. It was Dina DeNunzio, but I already knew that from the hair. Her strong, determined face looked scared and diminished. I hated seeing that.

"You kids?" she said, her voice wavery and weak. "What—what's going on?"

Before we could even start in on an answer, a big engine roared to life up in front of us, and then we were on the move—backward, which meant the trailer was on its way into the alley. And after that? Where were they taking us?

Think, for heaven's sake! It's obvious!

24

We helped Dina get free from the tarp. She sat up, her face real pale, and looked around, taking in the scene—interior of an eighteen-wheeler-type trailer containing a yellow cab, which provided the only light, and us kids. Dina's gaze rested on my face.

"Did you set me up?" she said.

"Huh?"

"Don't play dumb."

She's not playing.

I turned toward the taxi. "Shut up!"

"Are you telling me to shut up?" Dina said.

"No, no," I said, turning back to her in exasperation.

Dina's expression changed to one of puzzlement and maybe a bit of fear. "I'm talking about when you called me," she said, "to arrange the meeting at Joe Louis School."

"What about it?" I said, at the same time aware we

were now going forward and seemed to be picking up speed.

"Why did you do it?" Dina said.

"Why? Because we wanted to talk to you."

How about mentioning my father at this juncture in the narrative?

Now it was Ashanti's turn. She shouted toward the taxi, "Butt out!"

Dina stared at the taxi, seeing no one inside, of course, since Silas was lying on the front seat, out of view. She turned to Ashanti, gave her a long look.

"You can't hear that, can you?" Ashanti said.

"Hear you yelling butt out?" Dina replied. "I certainly can."

"Not that," Ashanti said. "I meant . . ." Her voice trailed off, and why not? Where were you supposed to begin?

Dina's eyes narrowed. "Are you kids on something?"

There was a silence. Then I started laughing, a totally weird thing to do at a time like that. Dina seemed to be on the point of getting angry at me, but at that point whoever was driving made a sharp turn, and we lost our balance and went sliding across the floor, caroming off the far side wall. We came to rest, all tangled up in each other and the tarp. For a moment my face was very close to Dina's.

"We called you," I said, "because we know there was

nothing accidental about Mr. Wilders's death. Which is what you suspected, right?"

"Maybe," Dina said, struggling to her feet. "I had questions. But what are you saying?"

We all rose, stood in a sort of circle, bracing ourselves against the motion of the trailer. "We're saying," I told her, "that they killed Mr. Wilders and just made it look like an accident."

"Who is they?" Dina said.

"A man named Kolnikov."

"Kirill Kolnikov?"

"We don't know his first name," I told her. "And this arsonist guy named Harry Henkel may have been in on it as well."

"But the point is they both work for Sheldon Gunn," Ashanti said.

"How do you know?" Dina said. "How do you know any of this?"

Don't mention the charm.

"Ashanti?" I said. "Do you think he's right?"

"Huh?" said Dina. "What's going on around here? Who are you talking about?"

"We'll show you," Ashanti said, and we all moved toward the cab. Ashanti pointed to Silas, now snoring on the front seat. "That's Silas."

"Right," said Dina. "I've seen him before. How can he sleep at a time like this?"

"First of all," I said, "Professor Wilders was his father. Second, he's not actually asleep."

"He got knocked out by the taxi driver," Ashanti added.

"Were you set up, too?" Dina said.

"Yeah," I told her, and described how we'd found her car abandoned at the sculpture park. "What happened to you?" I asked.

"I'm not really sure," Dina said. "I drove across the Brooklyn Bridge from Manhattan and ran into a detour just past the off-ramp. I ended up in Dumbo and pulled over to check my GPS. Then I heard something move in the backseat—whoever it was had been lurking there from the get-go. I started to turn, caught a glimpse of a man rising up, and that's the last thing I remember."

"What sort of man?" Ashanti said.

"Hard to say."

"Kind of rat-faced?" I said.

Dina nodded. "He was."

"That would be Henkel," I told her.

"Who is he, exactly?"

Do you really think there's time for all this explanation?

Ashanti reached into the car, gave Silas's foot a little shake. "Stop it right now," she said. "Wake up!"

"You think he's faking?" Dina said.

I totally am not.

"There's your answer," I said.

"I'm sorry?" said Dina.

Ashanti and I exchanged a look. "Should we tell her?" I said.

"Yes," Ashanti said

No way, you cretins!

"Tell me what?" Dina said.

I started to reach for the charm so I could show it to her, but just as I did, the truck made another sharp turn and we were all thrown across the floor again, excepting Silas, of course. The truck slowed down. Voices came from outside, but I couldn't make out the words. I heard a strange metallic sound—somewhere between a groan and a squeak—like massive hinges might make, and we bumped forward again; very slowly, I thought, but it was hard to tell with no outside view. We also seemed to be going down, perhaps on a steep hill or slope.

Brakes squeaked beneath us, and we came to a stop, the floor definitely slanting down. Somewhere up front, a door opened and closed: had the driver gotten out? I listened as hard as I could and was pretty sure I heard some squishy sorts of footsteps, like the ground was wet or muddy. And then silence.

We lay on the slanting floor of the trailer, all of us listening. Something landed on the roof with a smack. We gazed up at the ceiling. What would cause a smacking noise like that, a kind of thud followed by a hint of loose rattling? I had no idea. Then came another. And another. They seemed heavier than the first, even making the trailer shudder a bit.

"What's happening?" Dina said.

That was my question, too, but somehow it was disheartening to hear it from her lips first.

You blockheads! What do you think is happening? We're down at the bottom of a pit and it should be obvious where. They're going to bury us alive!

Dirt? That was dirt landing on the roof—*thump, thump, thump*?

"We've got to get out of here," Ashanti said. "That's earth coming down on us."

"Oh, my God," said Dina.

The next moment, we were struggling uphill toward the rear doors. Without a word—*thump, thump, thump* on the roof, coming faster—we all got some sort of grip on that lever thing and tried to move it. I took a quick peek at the charm: still warm, but other than that, nothing doing. I grunted away at the lever.

Not gonna happen. It's locked from the outside. Didn't you already prove that to yourselves?

We all let go except for Dina, who kept pushing and pulling at the lever. Buried alive! How long would it take for the four of us to breathe up all the oxygen in the trailer?

Thump, thump, thump: the thumps were still making the trailer shudder, but not as loud now. Why was that?

Because the layer of earth was building up on us, higher and higher?

Did the cabbie leave the keys in the ignition? When were you planning to check? Anytime soon?

"The keys!" I said.

"What are you talking about?" Dina said.

Ashanti was already sliding down the sloping floor to the taxi, like a surfer. She grabbed on to the driver's side door, peered inside.

"Yes!"

"Who's going to drive?" I said.

Before anyone could answer, Silas groaned and began to stir. His eyelids rose, fluttered closed, rose again. He looked at us, his eyes slowly coming into focus.

"Uh, what's going on?" he said. "Like, what's happenin', dudes?"

"You know perfectly well what's happening," Ashanti said.

"I do?" Silas started to sit up. "Oooh—my jaw hurts." He felt it gingerly. "Anybody got aspirin?"

I leaned in closer, gave him a real close look. Was he even sane? "You really don't know where you are?"

He glanced around. "We're in a cab. Who's paying? And where's the driver?"

"But you know more than we do!" Ashanti said. "You've been communicating nonstop."

"You're not making much sense, Ashanti. But no

change there, huh? Just kidding," he added, seeing the look on her face. That was when he noticed Dina, standing behind Ashanti. "What's she doing here? Where are we?"

Why didn't he know? Was the charmed, unconscious part of him—the part that had figured out so much already—completely separate from the rest of Silas? Or—maybe he'd been wrong about things, and we weren't getting buried alive, instead were—

"No time to explain," Dina said, her expression changing, turning more take-charge at last. "I'll handle the driving," she added, "unless anyone else is licensed."

Dina got behind the wheel of the taxi. Silas sat in front since he was already there, rooting around in the glove box for aspirin. Ashanti and I sat in back, right next to each other.

From above: *thump, thump, thump,* growing softer and softer. Dina switched on the engine, and also the headlights. It got bright in the trailer. Ashanti stuck her head out the window, peered up. "The roof's sagging."

"Buckle up," Dina said.

We buckled up.

Dina craned around so she could see through the rear window. "Get ready—I'm going to floor it. In reverse."

Dina floored it. She floored it so hard I would have

shot right into the front seat if it hadn't been for the seat belt. We shot straight backward—and up, on account of how the trailer was sloping—the tires shrieking, and the rear bumper of the taxi slammed into the locked double doors. They crumpled like tin foil, and we barreled out, seemed to be airborne for a second or two, and then came to a sudden and immediate stop, so violent I wanted to puke.

"Out, out, everybody out," Ashanti shouted, flinging open her door. I scrambled across the seat after her and jumped out, immediately sliding down a muddy slope and coming to rest near the back of the trailer.

It was a very strange world down where I was. For a few moments I could hardly make any sense of it at all. I lay in some sort of deep pit, lit strongly in some places and dimly in others by the taxi headlights. The rear of the taxi was embedded in the side of the pit and the front wheels weren't even on any sort of ground, but free in the air, the whole taxi now pointing upward. Tread marks led steeply up from the bottom of the pit, where the trailer stood, all the way up to the top. And there at the top, at the edge of the headlights' reach, two men were peering down. One, holding an umbrella, was Sheldon Gunn. The other, a gun in his hand, was Harry Henkel. Gunn motioned with his hand, and a bulldozer came into view, Kolnikov at the controls. He lowered the blade and dumped a load of dirt down into the pit, some of it landing on the roof of the trailer and some landing on us.

Dina turned to me, a clump of mud in her hair. "We're at the bottom of the construction site?"

"Yes. They're going to bury us way under Gunn Tower where no one will ever know."

"And not only that," Silas said, pointing out a wire that ran down the pit from the top and disappeared into a squarish hole in the dirt wall just beyond the trailer, about the size of my bedroom window, "they've found the Canarsee site, and they're going to blow it up."

"The Canarsee site?" Dina said.

"A sacred spring and burial place," Ashanti said.

"That Professor Wilders found," I added.

"Which was why"—Silas paused, took a deep breath—"they killed him."

Dina whipped out her phone, glanced at it and put it away. "No service."

"Jammed," I said. A shadow fell over us. I looked up. Another load of dirt was falling from above. "Quick," I said. We all rolled under the trailer. *Thud, thud, thud,* followed by a moment of quiet. Then I felt the charm heating up some more on my chest. Had it finally decided we were desperate enough? Was that how the charm thought? Were all charms this difficult? I took it off my neck. "If not now, when?" I said to it.

"Huh? said Dina. "What's that?"

"Uh, nothing," I said, now sounding my very dumbest. I pointed the charm—it actually pointed itself—at the wire.

25

Things happened fast after that. First came a sizzle and the wire burst into flame. Second, the flame, white hot, started racing up along the wire, growing bigger and bigger. It reached the top of the pit in a second or two and blew up in a strange silent burst that was too bright to look at. Then came cries of fear, followed by a deep rumbling. The whole pit began to cave in from the top down, sucking in Gunn, Henkel, and the bulldozer, with Kolnikov still in it. Terror spread across all their faces, making them look very similar, like brothers.

"Into the hole," I yelled, putting the charm back around my neck. "It's our only chance."

We all dove into the squarish hole. The walls of the pit came thundering down, and everything went dark. We were sealed in, down under the surface of the earth. I came real close to screaming in panic.

I took a deep breath, struggled for control of my own

self, suddenly found something useful to say. "Silas? Got your flashlight?"

"What kind of question is that?" He switched it on. I'd lost my glasses, but it didn't matter: I was in charmed vision mode now, everything hyperclear. I looked farther into the hole. We were in the Canarsee tunnel, the wire stretching on, out of sight: the remains of the wire, since the whole upper part was now gone. And in the other direction, outside the squarish window-sized hole, there was a small space, partly clear, saved from the cave-in by the trailer's bulk. Movement was going on in that cleared space, some sort of struggle involving three trapped men.

"Let's go," I said.

"Where?" said Silas.

I pushed him ahead into the tunnel, pushed them all. "Run!"

Ducking low, they all began to run, following Silas deeper into the tunnel. I glanced back through the squarish hole, saw Gunn claw himself out from a pile of dirt, then Kolnikov, and finally Henkel—all of them mud men now, like some alien species.

"Kill them!" Gunn shouted.

"But what about us?" Henkel said.

"We'll be rescued," Gunn told him. "And I'll do the thinking. Kill them all!"

Kolnikov switched on one of those cell phone

flashlights. Henkel took out his gun and started climbing into the squarish hole. I ran.

A gunshot rang out almost at once, very loud in the enclosed space. I ran as fast as I could, given I had to keep my head down in the tunnel—and my heart was running faster. Water was running, too: I could hear it flowing along beside me just beyond the right-hand tunnel wall, the old Canarsee spring that had been diverted long ago.

I caught up to the others, not too difficult since they weren't going very fast, not with Silas in the lead. Henkel's gun roared again, and a big lump of dirt fell from the tunnel wall, exposing a section of the huge old rusted pipe we'd seen before.

I heard Kolnikov behind us. "Give me this stupid gun," he said. "You shoot like blind man."

Which was the very moment Silas slipped on something and fell. We all slammed into him and went down in a heap just as Kolnikov fired. This shot probably would have hit us, but because we were on the ground, it missed, hitting the lower part of the pipe. A trickle of water dribbled out. I saw we'd fallen right beside the bones of the little family from long ago.

Before we could rise, Gunn, Kolnikov and Henkel came running up, stopping at the other end of the exposed pipe, water trickling out between us and them.

Gunn stared down at us, his eyes angry and wild. "Now," he said. "Do it."

Kolnikov raised the gun, pointed it at me first.

"Charm!" I cried out. "Please!"

Whether because of the charm or just the bullet hole, that was the moment the pipe erupted. An enormous tide of water gushed out with a pent-up sort of roar, missing the four of us by inches. But the flood didn't miss our enemies. It swept up Gunn, Kolnikov, and Henkel like they were nothing and carried them away. A hand grasped frantically above the wave tops before a whole big section of the roof fell in, turning everything to mud and entombing the three of them in an instant, deep and gone.

Water kept flowing out of the pipe, not as explosively as before but in growing volume. We jumped up, ran farther down the tunnel, the only direction possible. The water followed. At first we were splashing, then wading, and finally swimming, rising closer and closer to the ceiling in a shrinking blanket of air.

"I can't swim and hold the flashlight!" Silas shouted. The light flickered.

"Give it to me," Ashanti called.

"I can't swim anyway! I told you before!"

I rolled onto my back, the water so cold, and took off the charm. "Help," I said. But the charm had grown icy cold. What? We weren't desperate enough? "What's wrong with you?" Maybe I shouldn't have said that. The next moment, the charm broke into countless pieces, all of them fluttering out of my hand into the stream, and vanishing from sight. There was nothing I could do. We were on our own.

Silas's light flickered again. The thought *we're done* stirred in my mind, but before it could take over, a big fat length of pipe just ahead broke loose and bobbed away. Suddenly a hole appeared in the wall behind where that pipe section had been and we all got sucked into it.

Into the hole, and right away we got slammed into a narrow vertical shaft. Then the water came surging in and we rose and rose on a powerful sort of fountain top, like we were on an out-of-control elevator shooting up, up, up. High above, I glimpsed stars in the night sky, but just a small circle of them, crisscrossed by dark bars. A circle with dark bars? I squinted at it, but my normal lousy vision was back—thanks, charm—and I couldn't tell what I was seeing. The next second, the water, so much of it squeezed into the narrow shaft, enveloped me completely. I was going to drown! I closed my eyes, closed my mouth, held my breath. And all the time, I kept zooming upward at carnival-ride speed.

Then with a powerful whooshing sound, like a giant fire hose had been turned on, I was tossed out of the shaft and into the night. I tumbled in a somersault, gulping in air, and right beside me, also sort of tumbling, was a drain grate, round and crisscrossed with steel bars. I landed hard on wet ground, and the breath I'd just taken in got knocked right back out of me.

I sat up, panting, tried to get my bearings. Around me, Ashanti, Silas, and Dina, all of them soaked and bedraggled, were doing the same thing. We seemed to be in a bare sort of yard behind a plain concrete building that seemed familiar. On the other three sides stood a fence topped with razor wire. I gazed up at the windows on the back wall of the building.

The Annex? The offshoot or whatever it was of the Family Detention Center? Suddenly it made sense: wasn't the Annex very close to the Gunn Tower site? But on account of my blurry vision, I couldn't be sure. I squinted up at the window where I'd seen Tut-Tut.

"Tut-Tut! Tut-Tut!"

And almost like he'd been waiting for his cue, Tut-Tut popped up in the window.

"Tut-Tut!"

He waved through the window. Meanwhile water was rushing up from below, not just through the shaft but through the ground itself. Alarms and sirens started going off all over the place. The whole yard got flooded in seconds, dark water rising up and lifting us off the ground. In moments were already almost at second-floor level.

"Tut-Tut!" I called. "Jump!"

He started struggling with the window.

"Jump, jump!" Ashanti and Silas shouted.

"You know him?" said Dina, dog-paddling beside me, her hair no longer fluffy but clinging wetly to her head.

"No time to explain."

We treaded water. Somehow Silas's flashlight was still working. He shone it on Tut-Tut. Tut-Tut's face twisted with effort, and just when I thought he was never getting out, the window flew open. Tut-Tut climbed onto the sill, and did a beautiful swan dive into the water. Ashanti, Silas, and I swam over to Tut-Tut—Silas actually floundering more than swimming—and we surrounded him, pounding him on the back. Tut-Tut started to smile, but before that smile had finished spreading across his face, the earth roared and a whole ocean seemed to pour out of it. In an instant, we were caught in a sort of tsunami. It ripped that razor-wire fence right out of the ground and carried it away like nothing. We got swept out through the alley and onto the street. For a whole block, we were prisoners of this awesome tide, but then it began to lose its strength and finally deposited us—like shipwreck survivors on a beach—in front of a bar with a blinking neon light. A drunk peered out the window, gazed at us and the whole flood scene, shook his head, and retreated.

We got to our feet, soaked and shivering with cold.

"My God," Dina said. "I don't even know where to begin."

"Great," said Silas. "Then we'll be saying good night."

"Whoa," Dina said. "This is the story of my life." She turned to me. "How about we start with that thing you pointed at the detonation wire?"

Uh-oh. I tried to imagine the story Dina was going to put together, saw nothing good. "Let's make a deal," I said.

"What kind of deal?"

"The kind of deal where we answer your questions but you keep us out of the story."

"Huh?" said Dina. "How can I do that?"

"By making yourself the hero," Ashanti said.

Dina got a shrewd look in her eyes. "Let's hear it."

So we told her about the charm, where it had come from and what it had done.

"Who's going to believe that?" she said.

"Exactly," said Ashanti.

"Have we got a deal?" I said.

Dina nodded. We shook hands on it. She went one way. We went another.

First stop: Sherwood Street HQ, where we got the space heater going and dried ourselves out. Tut-Tut had a grin that wouldn't go away. Silas gave him the fake green card, and they high-fived each other, like all Tut-Tut's problems were solved. I was already making other plans.

We left Tut-Tut at HQ. Ashanti, Silas, and I went to the subway station, where she and I boarded our train, and Silas got on his. Not long after that, Ashanti and I were on our street, walking home on a nice normal sort of night, the sky clear, the air growing milder. I put my hand on her shoulder.

"I've got something to tell you," I said.

"Like what?"

I took a deep breath and told her the whole truth about what I'd seen and heard at Happy's Place. I felt better. She felt worse. Then I, too, felt worse.

"I'm home."

My mom called down from upstairs. "It's late. Were you at Ashanti's the whole time?"

"Yeah." In a manner of speaking, sort of stretching the point, most likely across the honesty/dishonesty line.

"I know it's still vacation, but you should have touched base."

"Sorry."

I threw all my mud encrusted clothes into the washer and took a shower. Just as I was getting into my pajamas, my mom knocked on the door.

"Did you hear about all the flooding downtown?" she said.

"Flooding?"

"A burst water main or something at the Gunn Tower site. The pictures are amazing."

"I'll, uh, check it out later."

I went into the bathroom and found my old glasses, the frames so lame and hideously out of date, with a prescription that was no longer strong enough but better than nothing. Just as a sort of test, I looked out the window. Up the street, a taxi was idling outside Ashanti's place. Her father came out, carrying a suitcase, and got in the taxi. It drove off.

Meanwhile my phone was ringing: Silas.

"Thaddeus thought it was for a TV show," he said.

"Huh?"

"Henkel paid him fifty bucks."

"I'm not following this, Silas."

"Meaning Thaddeus didn't know we were being set up. Henkel told him it was for this new reality show called *Scavenger Hunt* and Dina was one of the items."

"Thaddeus fell for that?"

"He's headed back to rehab first thing tomorrow."

The next morning Dina was on the front page of all the papers in town, and also on the *Today Show.* She told an exciting story about getting kidnapped because of her investigation into the death of Mr. Wilders, huge nighttime explosions at the Gunn Tower site, and the disappearance under a mountain of rubble of Sheldon Gunn and an unknown number of his associates. We kids weren't mentioned, not one word. A multi-acre lake—people were already calling it Lake Canarsee—was now forming at the Gunn Tower site. An architect showed preliminary plans for a boathouse and waterfront cafés.

It was a beautiful day, the sky clear, the sun warm for the middle of winter. I put on my backup glasses, and Ashanti and I took Pendleton for a walk. Ashanti was real quiet, her eyes all red-rimmed.

"My parents are getting divorced," she said in a lifeless kind of way.

"I'm really sorry."

"You're a good friend." A trace of a smile appeared on her face. "And so is Silas. He sent me flowers."

"I don't believe it."

"More like a photo of flowers, actually. As an e-mail attachment."

"You know what they say."

"It's the thought that counts?"

A few days later, I brought Tut-Tut home to meet my parents, step one in my plan. I prepared them with some facts, like his stutter, and not with some others, like his immigrant status. My parents were in a real good mood at the time. My mom had just found a job handling legal work for a nonprofit, and my dad had signed on for another George Gentry. There was talk of us buying the building from Mitch. We'd have lots of extra room.

"Mom? Dad? This is my friend Toussaint. Everyone calls him Tut-Tut."

"Pleased to meet you," said Tut-Tut, no hint of a stutter at all.

My mom and dad looked at me like I'd gone crazy. But I was sane. It was the charm that was sort of crazy, playing one last trick and saying good-bye in its own way.

Turn the page for a sample of the first book in the series . . .

THE OUTLAWS • OF • SHERWOOD STREET

Stealing from the Rich

1

At first I thought it all began with a foul—if an elbow to the head's not a foul, then what is?—but I figured out, maybe not as soon as I should have, that the beginning had come a little earlier. Just five or six hours, in fact, with me on my way to school and no time to lose. The second the doors of the subway car slid open, I jumped out, hurried along the platform, and took the stairs to street level two at a time. At the top, I was turning left, all set to run the block and a half to school, when I noticed something not right in front of the newsstand by the subway entrance. A homeless woman who'd been sitting outside for the past few weeks—HOMELESS, PLEASE HELP read the writing on the coffee cup she always held—was out there again, only now she'd tipped over and lay on her side. It must have just happened, because none of the people around—and there were lots—had gone to her yet. So I did.

I leaned over her. The woman was old, with white hair and a lined face, but maybe because her eyes were closed, I suddenly had this vision of how she'd looked as a young girl. She'd been really pretty. Something about that took away the fear I'd normally have had at such a moment.

"Are you all right?" I said.

Her eyes opened—blue eyes, but so faded there was hardly any color at all, except for the whites, which were crisscrossed with red veins. "Do I look all right?" she said, her voice surprisingly strong and not at all friendly.

I didn't know what to say.

Her eyes narrowed. "I know you," she said. "You're the girlie who dropped eighty-five cents in the cup. And sixty another time."

My parents said not to give money to street people, that there were better ways of helping, which maybe made sense but didn't feel right. So all I thought at that moment was: eighty-five cents and sixty cents—not much.

"Sorry," I said, "but that was all I had on me and—"

Before I could finish, strong hands were pushing me to the side and voices were calling "Get back, out of the way." Two cops had arrived and were clearing space around the woman. I ended up behind some tall people. An ambulance came roaring up, siren blaring. I caught glimpses of EMTs hopping out, feeling her pulse, clamping an oxygen mask over her face, rolling her onto a stretcher, and hoisting her into the back of the ambulance. The crowd lost interest fast, everyone dispersing, giving me a clear view, and what I saw was the woman's arm dangling down from the stretcher and something slipping off her wrist and falling into the gutter. I went forward and picked it up. It was a braided leather bracelet, possibly a charm bracelet, although only a single charm hung from it—a tiny silver heart.

"You dropped this," I called, just as the ambulance doors were closing. No one inside noticed me, except for the woman. Her eyes were looking right into mine and seemed to be trying to send some message, but I didn't get whatever it was. The doors slammed shut, and the ambulance took off. I ran a step or two after it before giving up. Then I put the charm bracelet in my pocket and hurried to school.

The foul I mentioned before happened after school on the basketball court, and real fast. Real fast was how things always happened on the basketball court, the mental part, too. Final seconds ticking down, Welland 18, Thatcher (that was us) 16, a typical score in the Independent School League, Seventh and Eighth Grade Girls Division, "independent" being a nicer way of saying "private." The games went by in blurs, partly because of the speed and partly because Dr. Singh, my ophthalmologist, didn't believe in fitting kids for contact lenses before they turned thirteen and I wasn't about to wear my stupid glasses on the court, since that meant wearing those even more stupid safety goggles over them. Did that mean I'd rather let my team down than look like a bug? If so, I'd have to live with it.

Back to the foul. In this particular blur, a component blur within the blur of the whole game, Ashanti, our tallest and best player, had intercepted a pass and cut across the key, a step ahead of number ten for Welland, who was even taller. But as Ashanti rose for the shot, number ten leaped, too, twisting in the air, elbow up, and that elbow caught Ashanti smack on the forehead. And right in front of the ref, a chinless guy with sharp, darting eyes whom I'd seen around the neighborhood but couldn't place at that moment. Right in front of his sharp, darting eyes: impossible to miss, but no whistle, no call. What was up with that?

"Hey!" I yelled.

Oops. Yelling at the ref was a complete no-no, also a technical, and in all the years I'd been playing basketball, now almost three, I'd never heard a player do it. But it was so obvious! And wrong! The ref didn't seem to have heard my yell—he was missing everything, an equal-opportunity goof-up—and meanwhile things were happening, such as Ashanti starting to fall, the ball coming loose, and big number ten turning to chase after it. Somehow the ball came bouncing right into my hands, out in three-point land.

"Shoot, Robbie, shoot!" That was the coach, Ms. Kleinberg, shouting at me from the bench. She'd played for Dartmouth and even tried out for the Olympic team, getting cut in training camp. Ms. Kleinberg had a fantastic shot; I'd seen her hit forty-seven in a row from the free-throw line. But shooting wasn't my thing. Passing was my thing. I always looked to pass the moment I got the ball.

But no one was open, at least no one in my field of vision—not a very clear field, on account of my unaided eyesight, minus three in the right, minus two-point-five in the left.

"Shoot!"

I just stood there, felt a sweat smear on the ball, not mine, since I hadn't yet worked up a sweat. This was actually the first time I'd touched the ball in the second half. I was a seventh-grader and new to Thatcher and not a starter, and also didn't deserve to start—don't get me wrong about that. In the first half, I'd come in with about five minutes left, made two successful passes, and been called once for traveling, probably adding up to my best performance of the season, so far. For some reason, Ms. Kleinberg had decided to push her luck and send me back in at the end of the game, crunch time. Since then, I'd mostly been running up and down the floor, never too far from the ball but also never a factor. I was fine with that; I liked running.

Number ten closed in.

"Two seconds! Robbie! Shoot!"

Two seconds? Not a good moment for weird distractions to be happening, but a weird distraction was happening: suddenly my head hurt, my forehead, in the exact same spot where number ten had elbowed Ashanti. Was *pain* even the right word? This . . . *feeling,* maybe a better name, was like a tiny low-powered electric ball. It seemed to be pressing just behind my forehead, pressing, pressing, and then with no warning, two tiny electric currents seemed to emerge, one hooking up to each eye, and the pain, or feeling, vanished immediately. And all at once, my vision cleared, and I could see perfectly, more clearly than at any time in my life, every detail sharp and focused! And not only that—

Number ten was almost on me, her long arms up, hands high.

"Shoot!"

And not only that, but I saw—or thought I saw, since it was so impossible—the strangest thing: a narrow beam of light, reddish light, very faint, with golden highlights, that seemed to glow right out of my eyes. It shaped a long, rising arc, then sloped down into the basket, dead center. Somehow I knew it was no longer a matter of shooting the ball—normally so big and unmanageable—but simply lofting it up onto that red-gold glowing beam. So I did, just lofted the ball onto the beam. The beam vanished at once, and then there was only the ball, soaring over number ten's outstretched hands, curving through the air with lots of backspin, just like a shot launched by someone who knew what she was doing, and then—*swish*. Nothing but net, from three-point land.

Bbbbzzzz. The buzzer buzzed. Game over. Thatcher 19, Welland 18. A buzzer beater? I'd just won the game with a buzzer beater, like in the kind of daydream fantasy I didn't even have anymore, at least when it came to sports. The kids were around me now, pretty pumped, although not too pumped, which seemed to be the Thatcher way.

We went into the locker room. In my old school, PS 501, the Joe Louis School, there hadn't been a locker room—the kids made do with the bathroom near the gym—but the Thatcher girls' locker room was nice, with a steam bath, individual shower stalls, fluffy white towels.

Ms. Kleinberg patted me on the back. "Nice job," she said. "More, more, more."

"Um," I said, giving Ms. Kleinberg a careful look.

Now that the excitement, what there'd been of it, had died down, I had a chance to think, *Hello? That beam, red and gold? Anybody?* But nobody said a word about it. Meaning no one else saw it except me? Whoa.

"No foul?" said Ashanti, kicking off her shoes. "Is he blind or something?"

"That's life," said Ms. Kleinberg, handing her an ice pack. "Have a good weekend, everybody. Practice Monday." She went into her office.

Ashanti sat in front of her locker, dropped the ice pack on the floor, gave me what seemed like an angry look. "An elbow in the head is life?"

"Does it hurt?" I said.

"What do you think?" said Ashanti.

Ashanti was intimidating, but a question I thought was important had occurred to me, so I pressed on. "Does it feel kind of like a tiny electric ball?"

Ashanti squinted at me in a scary way. "Huh? Is that supposed to be funny?"

"No," I said. "No, no." I moved to my own locker, which looked out of focus, meaning my vision was back to normal. I took out my glasses and put them on. Very cool glasses from the Smith Street Eyeware Boutique, one of the coolest opticians in Brooklyn, which probably meant in the whole world, but I hated them. Other ophthalmologists handed out contacts left and right. How come I got stuck with Dr. Singh? And as for the red-gold beam, either some new eye screwup was in the mix, or I'd imagined it. What other explanation was there? No one had seen it: therefore, not real. The imagination played tricks on you. That was one of my dad's big beliefs. He was writing a novella about it, or possibly a memoir.

I closed my locker, glimpsing my face in the mirror that hung on the inside of the door. Nonna—the name for Grandma that my grandmother on my mother's side had finally chosen for herself, after tryouts for Mummy-mum, Nana, and Gretchen (her given name)—had gazed at me on her last visit (she lived in Arizona and didn't visit often) and said, "She'll be a beautiful woman, one day." Kind of a mystery who Nonna had been addressing, since there'd been just the two us in the room, but that wasn't the point. The point: was this supposed day coming anytime soon, the day of my beauty revealed for all to see? No sign of it yet. I clicked the combination into the locked position and was turning to leave when I felt a strange warmth in my pocket. I reached in and took out the braided bracelet. The tiny silver heart was more than warm—in fact, almost too hot to touch. My locker was near the heating vent: maybe that was the explanation. But that silver heart was kind of pretty. I slipped the bracelet on my wrist.

• • •

Home was two subway stops away, but it was a nice day—nice for winter, meaning sunny, not too cold, and none of that wind funneling through the gaps between buildings and down the streets, like icy invisible streams—so I started walking. Twenty-two blocks—twenty-five if I took a detour past Joe Louis—from the edge of one cool neighborhood, where the adults looked a lot like my parents, through the main portion of the walk where they did not, and finally to the edge of another cool neighborhood, mine, where they did again. The difference wasn't skin color—Ashanti, for example, lived practically across the street from me—or the manner of dress, although that was part of it; it was more something else, some attitude thing, much harder to define.

I passed some nice brownstones, the fixed-up kind with freshly painted trim, nothing crumbling, plants in the windows. Two nannies stood in front of one of them, each push-pulling on a stroller, back and forth, back and forth, in a machinelike way. The babies slept, one drooling, one not. Then came a grocery store with brightly colored fruit in the window, all arranged in neat rows. I crossed the street to the first block where walking at night wasn't a good idea, passing a boarded-up building, a warehouse, an old greasy sofa in the gutter. A veiled woman with just a little slit to see through went past, her dark eyes lighting on me for a moment. Rowdy boys on bikes blew by, fluttering the veiled woman's robe. My backpack got heavier—there was homework at Thatcher, lots—but I turned left at the next corner and took the detour anyway. Not that I liked going by Joe Louis, exactly; it was more a matter of just being drawn to it.

It was past dismissal by the time I reached my old school, a brick and glass building of no distinction, very different from Thatcher, which was a grand nineteenth-century affair on the outside, bright and modern on the inside, thanks to the work of a famous architect who was also an alum; there were lots of famous alums from Thatcher.

Some of the kids from my neighborhood got sent to private school right from kindergarten; others made the switch later—third grade, maybe, or fifth. But the plan had always been for me to be a public school kid from start to finish; my parents believed in public schools. "Just wait," some of their friends had said. I'd heard that plenty of times. My parents had waited and waited and then been in the very last group to cave. Nothing I said or did had budged them, and I'd thrown everything I'd had at them, emptied out the cupboard of bad behavior. "Your friends from Joe Louis will still be your friends," they'd told me. Which had already turned out to be false. And "Don't worry—you'll make new friends at Thatcher." Which hadn't happened yet, most of the Thatcher kids having been there together for years. Didn't mean it wouldn't happen, I told myself, stopping by the chain-link fence and gazing through at the small, paved school yard with its single backboard, no net on the basket, windblown trash and broken glass heaped in the corners.

No one was shooting hoops. There was only one person around, a kid I'd seen in the halls. What did they call him? Tut-Tut? Yes, that was it, on account of his stutter. He'd arrived from—Where was it? Haiti?—two or three years before, a scrawny kid with modified dreads and a sweet face. Right now he was squatting down on the pavement just a few feet from the fence, drawing with chalk. Tut-Tut didn't seem to notice me at all; I could feel his concentration. He shifted around a little, and I saw what he was drawing.

Hey! It was beautiful: a red bird, maybe a parrot, with a green head and yellow eyes, so lifelike that it looked as though it could actually fly off the pavement at any moment.

"It's great," I said.

Tut-Tut glanced up, startled. He almost tipped over backward.

"Is it based on a real bird?" I said.

Tut-Tut's mouth opened, and his lips moved a bit, like he was forming a word, but no sound came out.

"Or did you just make it up?" I said.

"N-n-n-," said Tut-Tut. "T-t-t-th-th-th-th . . ." He went silent.

"It's real?" I said.

"T-t-t-t-th-th-th-th-the b-b-b-bb-bb-bbb-bbbb-bbbbb-bbbbbb . . ." He went silent again, took a deep breath, and nodded yes.

A real parrot, meaning it had a name, maybe a parrot he'd seen in Haiti, or even kept in a cage. I had lots of follow-up questions, but I didn't have the heart to watch Tut-Tut trying to answer them. Plus, that strange pressure ball thing in my head was back, not electrical and powerful like on the basketball court, more just letting me know it was there.

Tut-Tut licked his lips. "W-," he began. "W-w-w-w-w-w-w-wh-wh-wh—"

The pressure thing grew. And the more Tut-Tut tried to say whatever it was he wanted to say, the stronger it got. "W-wh-wh-wha-wha-wha-wha-wha—" Now I felt the electrical component, and my vision started going funny. My imagination playing tricks? I took off my glasses, watched the world grow clearer.

"Wh-wha-wha-wh-wh-wh-w-w-w-w . . ." Tut-Tut gave up.

And the moment he gave up, my vision began deteriorating back to normal. The pressure in my head vanished. I put on my glasses. If this was my imagination, it was suddenly getting good at tricks. The streetlights went on.

"I better get going," I said.

Was I coming down with something? I took off my glove and touched my forehead; it felt cool. And in fact I felt fine all over, head to toe, the way you do after running around for a while. There were also growing pains to factor in: lots of possible explanations for something that would probably never happen again. "Anyway, cool bird," I said.

Tut-Tut grunted.

I walked off. A block away, waiting for the light to change, I felt the silver heart. It had heated up again, but now cooled quickly under my touch. The light changed. I glanced back. The school yard was empty.